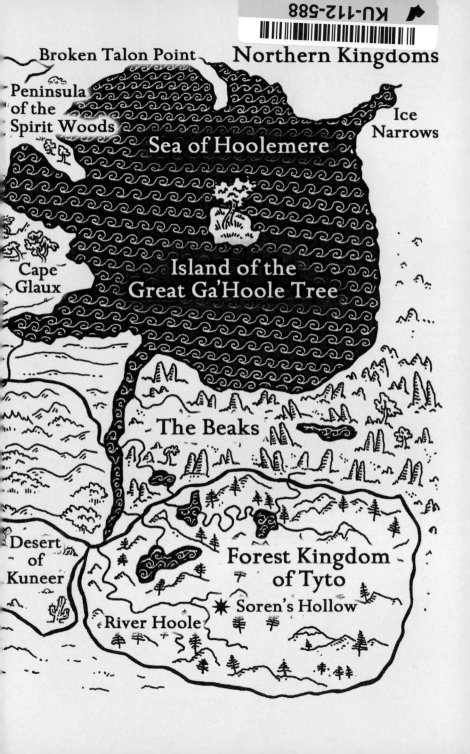

KU-112-588

The Guardians of Ga'Hoole Series:

GUARDIANS
OF GA'HOOLE

BOOK FIVE

The Shattering

Kathryn Lasky

HarperCollins *Children's Books*

First published in the USA by Scholastic Inc 2004
First published in Great Britain by HarperCollins *Children's Books* 2007
HarperCollins *Children's Books* is a division of HarperCollins*Publishers* Ltd
77-85 Fulham Palace Road, Hammersmith, London W6 8JB

The HarperCollins *Children's Books* website address is
www.harpercollinschildrensbooks.co.uk

Text copyright © Kathryn Lasky 2004
Illustrations copyright © Richard Cowdrey 2004

The author and illustrator assert the moral right to be identified as the author
and illustrator of this work

ISBN-13 978-0-00-721521-8

Conditions of Sale
This book is sold subject to the condition that it shall not, by way of trade or
otherwise, be lent, re-sold, hired out or otherwise circulated without the
publisher's prior written consent in any form of binding or cover other than
that in which it is published and without a similar condition including this
condition being imposed on the subsequent purchaser.

Mixed Sources
Product group from well-managed
forests and other controlled sources
www.fsc.org Cert no. SW-COC-001806
© 1996 Forest Stewardship Council

FSC is a non-profit international organisation established to promote the
responsible management of the world's forests. Products carrying the FSC
label are independently certified to assure consumers that they come
from forests that are managed to meet the social, economic and
ecological needs of present and future generations.

Find out more about HarperCollins and the environment at
www.harpercollins.co.uk/green

For Joy Peskin

ROTHERHAM LIBRARY SERVICE	
B53034948	
Bertrams	26/11/2012
JF	£8.99
KIM	

Eglantine and Primrose sliced through the clear
space between two blazing trees.

It was the same. That was her first thought.

It looks just like the old fir tree, the one where Soren and I were hatched. And even the shape of the hollow's opening where Mum and Da made their nest, a lopsided O – wasn't that the exact shape?

Eglantine knew she was dreaming, but it seemed so real. Like no dream she'd ever had. It was so lovely she didn't want it to end. She wondered if she flew a little closer and just took a peek, would the hollow look the same inside? Would her mum and da be there? Oh, it had been forever since she'd seen them. Soren said they were dead. He had seen their scrooms, the spirits of dead owls. She hated it when Soren said that. Eglantine squirmed now in her sleep as the words from the awful conversation wove through her dream.

"You saw their scrooms? That means they are dead, doesn't it, Soren?"

"It does, Eglantine, and there is nothing we can do about that."

And then Twilight had added his horrible conclusion. *"Dead is dead."*

"Dead is dead." The words swirled around her like black crows getting ready to mob. *"Dead IS NOT dead!"* She shouted back in her dream. *"Dead IS NOT dead."*

CHAPTER ONE

A friend in Need?

"Wake up, Eglantine! Wake up!" Primrose, Eglantine's hollowmate, was vigorously shaking her. "You're just having a bad dream."

"Oh, for Glaux's sake, let her sleep," said Ginger, the newest hollowmate. Ginger was a Barn Owl who had actually been part of the attacking forces during the terrible siege of the previous winter. She had been wounded, but during her recovery she had decided that she'd had enough of the Pure Ones and much preferred life in the Great Ga'Hoole Tree. She had not yet, of course, been approved for training as a Guardian. That would require some time. Nonetheless, Eglantine had taken her under her wing, so to speak, and become a kind of big sister to Ginger during her recovery. They had grown quite close in the process. But Primrose was still Eglantine's best friend in the tree.

"Let her sleep?" Primrose swivelled her head towards the reddish Barn Owl. "Let her continue to have this awful dream?"

Ginger merely sighed and said, "She's tired. She needs her sleep, bad dream or not."

Suddenly Eglantine's eyes flicked open. "Why in the name of Glaux are you shaking me? I was having the loveliest dream."

"Loveliest dream?" *Has she lost her mind?* thought Primrose. "You were screaming your head off about being dead or not dead, Eglantine."

Eglantine blinked. "No I wasn't," she replied defiantly. "I was having a wonderful dream about the old hollow in the fir tree back in Tyto where Soren and I lived with our mum and da. And I was just about to go into the hollow. Something wonderful was about to happen, and then you came along and shook me." She looked accusingly at Primrose. Ginger pretended she wasn't paying any attention and commenced humming a little owl ditty that Eglantine had taught her.

Now it was Primrose who blinked at Eglantine. Something about her friend seemed different. *She's seemed different for a while*, Primrose thought. *Is it just my imagination? It must be my imagination. What if she doesn't want to be my friend any more?* Primrose didn't think she could stand that. She had to stop thinking this way. She and Eglantine were best friends. They had been from the very start, from the day Eglantine had been rescued. Why, she herself had been on the rescue mission that had found Eglantine.

Like most of the young owls in the Great Ga'Hoole Tree, Primrose had also been rescued by the Guardians. She had lost everything in a devastating fire that had swept through the forest of Silverveil. In a matter of minutes her hollow, her homeland, her parents and even the eggs of her future brothers and sisters had been destroyed. But since her rescue, life at the Great Ga'Hoole Tree had been wonderful, and the best part was having a best friend. It didn't matter that she was a Pygmy Owl, quite small, and that Eglantine, a Barn Owl, was huge by comparison. They had so much in common. They were so much alike. No, she'd never find another friend like Eglantine.

"Look," she said to Eglantine, "I'm sorry I woke you from your nice dream. It looked like a nightmare to me. I just couldn't stand hearing you cry like that."

"It's all right, Primrose, don't worry. I know you meant well." Eglantine said it softly, and then repeated, "Don't worry. I'm going right back to sleep and finish my nice dream."

But Primrose *was* worried.

Within a few minutes it would be tween time, those slivers of seconds between the last minute of the day and the first of the evening. It was a lovely time, especially in summer as it was now. The sky turned a soft lavender just as the sun began to slip away. Sometimes there were streaks of pink and a fragile light illuminated every leaf and blade of grass, making everything stand out with special beauty. Primrose sat on the branch just outside her hollow and watched the subtle transformation of the lovely Island of Hoole as the light played across it. How close they had come last winter to losing it all to the terrible owls known as the Pure Ones, who were led by Kludd, the brother of Eglantine and Soren.

How fragile life is, thought Primrose, *how fragile everything is, including friendship*. And once more she felt a tremor deep within her gizzard, where all owls feel their most intense feelings.

She could not dwell upon this, she realised. She was now up for the evening, and the rest of the tree would soon be up as well. Perhaps she would go to the library. It was summertime and there were fewer chaw practices and classes, so she could pick out a book and read just for fun – a nice joke or riddle book. Nothing too serious, like colliering techniques, weather interpretation (which the owls of the great tree were expected to be familiar with) or land and celestial navigation, which Primrose, being a member of the search-and-rescue chaw, was expected to know. No, not tonight.

Tonight, she would find herself a really good joke book and she would laugh as loud as she wanted because there would be no one else in the library at this early hour of the evening.

CHAPTER TWO

Spronk No More

But Primrose was not to be alone.

"I just don't understand it Digger," Otulissa said in a low, rasping whisper as Primrose entered the library. "If it hadn't been for Dewlap, Strix Struma would never have been killed. She's a traitor, I tell you."

"Look, I agree that she's a traitor but we would have had that battle with the Pure Ones any way you look at it," Digger said. "Primrose, you're up early," he added, seeing her come into the library.

"Yeah, couldn't sleep," Primrose lied. "You're talking about what's going to happen to Dewlap?"

"Yes, and as far as we can see, nothing's going to happen to her," Otulissa huffed. "It just isn't fair."

"They say," Primrose offered, "that she's had a nervous breakdown. That she's really sick and didn't know what she was doing."

"Breakdown my flight feathers!" Otulissa harrumphed. "And I'll tell you what she was doing." Otulissa didn't wait for them to ask. "She was not only leaking information to the enemy and destroying books, she was also hoarding."

"Hoarding!" both Primrose and Digger said at once.

"Hoarding what?" Digger asked. "What possibly could there have been to hoard last winter?"

"I'll tell you what: while we all were starving during that long siege, she had her own private supply of milkberries and Ga'Hoole nuts. You didn't see her getting any thinner last winter while the rest of us were so pathetically skinny we could have slipped through a knothole."

"I can already do that," Primrose said, trying to make a small joke. After all, she had come here to read a joke book. She had not expected such serious conversation.

"Oh, sorry," Otulissa replied. "I wasn't talking about Pygmy Owls, but you got awfully skinny yourself, Primrose. Probably could have slipped into a hummingbird hole."

"What are you reading, Otulissa?" Primrose asked, hoping to lighten the mood.

"*Dowsing and divining techniques for metals and water.* There's a short chapter in here by Strix Emerilla. You know, my ancestor—"

"The renowned weathertrix," Primrose finished the sentence. They all knew about Otulissa's ancestor Strix Emerilla. There was hardly a word written by her that Otulissa hadn't read, and she rarely missed an opportunity to remind them of her connection to the great owl. But Primrose didn't mind. She was happy that Otulissa was showing signs of being herself again.

"That's terrible, about the hoarding," Digger said. "I never knew that. I wonder what the parliament will decide about Dewlap." Then he looked slyly at Otulissa. "Have you been to the roots lately?"

Very few of the owls knew about the roots, but Primrose had once overheard the band – as Soren, Gylfie, Twilight and Digger were often called – talk about them. Of course, they had immediately sworn her to secrecy. The place they called 'the roots' was a cramped space deep under the Great Ga'Hoole Tree directly beneath the parliament chamber. Something about the tangled roots and ceiling timbers caused sounds to resonate, most particularly the sounds coming from the owls' innermost parliament chamber. The roots transmitted the voices of the owls in the parliament above. Listening in on closed parliament sessions was the only really bad thing that the band, plus Otulissa, ever did. It was out-and-out eavesdropping. They all knew it. They all felt guilty about it. But they simply couldn't stop. They had a million and one ways of rationalising their snooping activities, but their excuses never made them feel much better. Still, they continued to secretly listen.

"I just don't buy it – the stuff about Dewlap having a nervous breakdown: she's not shattered."

"Shattered?" Digger and Primrose both said at once.

"Shattering. It's terrible when it happens, worse than any moon blinking that Soren and Gylfie went through at St Aggie's, believe me."

"How could anything be worse than moon blinking?" Digger wondered aloud.

"Well, shattering is. I read about it in that book, *Fleckasia and Other Disorders of the Gizzard*, which we have Dewlap to thank for confiscating and then losing."

"Well, what is it? Did you read enough to learn anything about it?" Digger asked.

"A little bit." Otulissa's plumage suddenly drooped and flattened. She was 'wilfing'. This happens to owls when they experience extreme fear or agitation.

Primrose blinked. *Shattering must be awful*, she thought, *if just reading about it does this to Otulissa.*

"You see," Otulissa continued, regaining some of her composure. "Moon blinking is caused by the moon – especially the full moon – shining down upon the head of a sleeping owl, resulting in massive disorientation and confusion of one's sense of self. But shattering is much worse. It is not caused by the moon but by exposure to flecks under certain conditions."

"You mean like when we infiltrated St Aggie's and discovered that the Pure Ones' agents were putting flecks into the nests in the eggorium?" Digger asked.

"Yes, precisely. When owls are still in the egg it can happen. Young owls in general are very susceptible. But it is thought that shattering can happen to almost any owl."

"But look at all the flecks at St Aggie's," Digger said. "When we were there, we weren't hurt by them. It was the moon blinking that was bad."

"I know it's very odd. Sometimes, I guess, one can rub right up against flecks and it doesn't cause shattering. Like with Hortense from Ambala. They say that the streams of Ambala have lots of flecks. But she wasn't shattered. Instead she simply has deformed wings and is small for her age. It's a very complicated thing. If only that stupid old Burrowing Owl Dewlap – no offence, Digger..." she apologised because Digger himself was a Burrowing Owl, "...but if only she hadn't taken that book."

"But aren't there other books in the library that might tell about it – about shattering?" Primrose asked. "I mean now that nothing is spronk any longer."

"Not so far and believe me, I have scoured this library."

Books being declared spronk had been the beginning of Otulissa's problems with Dewlap, indeed the beginning of all of their problems with the strange old Burrowing Owl who was the Ga'Hoolology ryb. Spronk meant forbidden and nothing, especially books, had ever been forbidden at the Great Ga'Hoole Tree. Then for some reason Dewlap had forbidden the young owls access to certain books. No one had really agreed with her, and Ezylryb had personally delivered the fleckasia book to Otulissa. But then Dewlap had confiscated and lost it.

At that moment a matron, a rather chubby Short-eared Owl, stuck her head in the library. "Almost time for tweener," she hooted cheerfully. Tweener was their evening meal, just as breaklight was their morning meal and the last food they consumed before going to sleep for the day.

So the three owls made their way to the dining hollow.

CHAPTER THREE

A Grim Tweener

Primrose stopped in her own hollow to check if Eglantine had got up. She'd become a late sleeper lately, which was strange because it was summertime and the nights were so short that every owl wanted to be flying about having larks in the dark. With no heavy study or chaw schedule, flying on the smooth air of warm nights under the great summer constellations was so much fun that no owl wanted to miss a minute of the blackness. Primrose was pleased to see that the hollow was empty and that Eglantine and Ginger would not be late to the dining hollow as they so often were. She smelled good things as she approached. Could it be barbecued bat wings? Bats were common summer food. Fruit bats in particular were thick around the Great Ga'Hoole Tree in the early part of the summer evenings. It could hardly be called hunting as an owl only had to stick its head out of a hollow opening to catch one on the wing.

Primrose made her way to her usual spot at Mrs Plithiver's table. The nest-maid snakes of the Great Ga'Hoole Tree also served as dining tables for the owls. They stretched their supple, rosy-scaled bodies to accommodate at least half a dozen owls for dining. But now as Primrose approached, she saw that Mrs P's table was overcrowded and the place where she usually sat next to Eglantine was taken by Ginger. Soren waved a wing for her to come over, anyway.

"There's always room dearie," Mrs P said. She stretched herself a bit more and all the owls squashed in a little closer. All the owls, that is, except Eglantine and Ginger, who continued jabbering away to each other in low whispers.

Soren blinked. He was shocked at his sister's rude behaviour. "Eglantine! Could you stop talking for one second and move your butt feathers to make room for Primrose?"

"Oh dear. Sorry Prim." Eglantine looked up and began to move over.

But Soren was still angry. He blinked and looked at Eglantine and then Ginger. "You know Eglantine, whispering at the table isn't very polite. If you have something that is so private that the rest of us can't hear it, maybe you should eat by yourselves."

What, Primrose wondered, *could Eglantine and Ginger have to say that was so private?* Primrose suddenly realised that Ginger was often trying to get Eglantine alone, not just away from her but from the group. Was Ginger jealous of all of Eglantine's friends? True, they were all in training to be Guardians, and she knew how much Ginger hoped to be approved for training too. Did Ginger think that Eglantine would have some special influence over that approval?

There was an awkward silence, and then Eglantine and Ginger erupted into convulsive laughter as if sharing a very private joke. The other owls looked on grimly, but Primrose wilfed in the biggest way and became so slender that there was hardly any need for anyone to squash in. She just knew they were laughing about her, or thinking how she wouldn't understand their little joke anyway. To think that just last evening she had looked for a joke book. *Well, the joke's on me*, she thought sourly.

To change the subject, Soren began talking about the weather experiments that Ezylryb wanted him to do. "Martin can't go and neither can Ruby because they are doing other experiments for him. That's why he said I could ask friends from other chaws for help. So Twilight and Gylfie and Digger are going. You want to go, Otulissa?"

"No I can't," she replied. "I have to run that experiment on the far beach for him."

"Ginger and I will go," Eglantine piped up.

"You have to be full-fledged chaw members, and you're still in training, Eglantine. I don't think he'd agree. What about you Primrose? You're full-fledged. Want to go?"

"No, not tonight," she answered quietly. She knew that if she got to go and Eglantine didn't, it would drive an even deeper wedge in their friendship.

"Come on, Soren. Go ask Ezylryb," Eglantine urged her brother.

"No, I'm not going to bother him when I know what the answer will be."

"That frinks me off," Eglantine said sourly.

"Well, too bad." Soren saw Ginger give Eglantine a nudge and whisper something in her ear.

"Young'uns!" Mrs P interrupted. "No bad language, not at the table, please. And need I remind you, I am the table!"

Tweener, usually a cheerful meal, was not going well. Now Gylfie, in another attempt to change the subject, reminded everyone that on the next evening Trader Mags would be arriving. "Trader Mags always comes on the first day of full shine in the summer," she said.

"Why's that?" Primrose asked, relieved to be talking about something other than Eglantine's rude behaviour.

"She thinks the full moon shows off her wares best," Soren said.

"As if the tawdriness of all that frippery needs any more sparkle," Otulissa said acidly. Otulissa did not approve of Trader Mags.

"Who's Trader Mags?" Ginger asked.

"You don't know about Trader Mags?" Eglantine blinked. "Ooh, she brings the most wonderful stuff. We'll have so much fun looking at it together. Shopping!"

Primrose sensed a wilfing in her gizzard.

"Trader Mags," Otulissa said in a very haughty, superior voice, "is an ostentatious magpie who – true to her nature – is quite skilful at 'collecting' a variety of items. 'Collecting' is, of course, a euphemism for what some might call stealing."

"Ooh!" Ginger exclaimed again, her eyes blinking darkly in anticipation. "Where does she get the stuff?"

"The Others – their old ruins, their churches or castles, what have you," Otulissa continued. "Bits of stained glass, broken crockery, beads and baubles – all the colourful, garish doodads that the Others seem to have loved. Tawdry, awful stuff, in my opinion."

"Madame Plonk likes it," Eglantine said, cheerfully undeterred by Otulissa's sneering tone.

"She would," Otulissa said. "Madame Plonk is hardly known for her restraint in matters of style. There's a touch of the tawdry in that Snowy Owl, to say the least." Otulissa sniffed. "One might even say she's an exhibitionist."

"Come off it, Otulissa," Twilight, the huge Great Grey, scoffed. "Look, we can't all be as pure as you."

Silence fell on the table like a blade slashing through the chatter. Since the siege and their fierce battle with the Pure Ones, something had happened to the word 'pure', as if it had become a swear word overnight. Soren felt Mrs P squirm and the owls' Ga'Hoole-nut cups of milkberry tea trembled slightly. Ezylryb's words from the Last Ceremony for Strix Struma following her death in battle came back to him:

We have been fighting a war that has been instigated by this vile notion that declares that some breeds of owls are better than others, more pure. Not one of us shall, I suppose, ever again say the words 'pure' or 'purity' without thinking of the bloodshed these words have caused. How unfortunate that a good word has been ruined by the evilness of one group.

Twilight, realising too late what he had just said, clamped his beak shut.

Knowing how mortified Twilight must feel, Otulissa tried to set things to rights again. "Oh, I have never been all that comfortable with fancy stuff. Madam Plonk's voice is so beautiful when she sings, and she herself is so lovely to look at, I feel she needs no further adornment. And such ornamentation would be completely wasted on me."

It had been a gracious speech until this point, but then for some reason that eluded even Otulissa, she swivelled her head towards Ginger. "Just give me my helm, my nickel-alloy battle claws and a burning branch, and I feel adorned." The glare in the young Spotted Owl's yellow eyes was harsh. It had been in just such battle gear that Otulissa had served with great bravery in one of the fiercest encounters with the Pure Ones.

Once more silence settled on the table, thickly this time, like fog that wouldn't burn off.

A wet poop joke, that's what we need, Soren thought desperately.

"Did you hear the one about the seagull that got hit by the wet poop of a bat?" Often, wet poop jokes began with seagulls, for they were considered the worst and messiest of the wet poopers.

"No, what's that?" said Gylfie, equally desperate to lift the mood.

"Well, this seagull got hit right in the eyes by an off-loading bat and could hardly see to fly. And the bat turned around and said, 'Now you're as blind as a splat!'"

The table roared with the *churring* sound of owl laughter. A little too hard, Soren thought, for the joke was not that funny. He nervously looked down at Mrs P because they had just violated one of the few rules of the dining hollow – no wet poop jokes at meals. Nest-maids were under strict orders to writhe at the first words of a wet poop joke and throw everything off the table and send the owls scattering. But Mrs P was as still as could be. She must have been as desperate as the rest of them to change the subject once the dreadful word had been mentioned.

Everyone continued to *churr* and guffaw. Soren noticed that other tables began to look at them as loose feathers from the laughing owls drifted down.

But then he swivelled his head towards Primrose and caught his breath when he saw her. *Glaux! Is she laughing or crying?* The little Pygmy was shaking hard and making unintelligible sounds, but there were tears streaming from her eyes.

CHAPTER FOUR

A Missing Piece

"You see, Eglantine," Ginger was saying back in the hollow, "just one more way you're being left out."

"I know. It's getting bad. And did I tell you how Soren missed my first Fur-on-Bones ceremony?"

"No, you don't say! I am shocked. Your own brother didn't come to your Fur-on-Bones ceremony? That's unforgivable."

"He had some excuse, but he was really out larking about with the band."

"The band?"

"That's what everyone calls the four of them – Soren, Gylfie, Twilight and Digger – because they all came here together, and they stick together."

"And leave you out!"

"Right! I've never felt more left out in my life."

You feel left out?! What about me? Primrose almost screamed from the branch she was perched on just outside the hollow. She was eavesdropping. She knew it wasn't very nice, but it was her hollow too after all, and they wouldn't talk this freely if they knew she were around.

"Do you know what I think you should do about it?" Ginger asked.

"What?"

Primrose inclined her head a bit more so she could hear better.

"Well," Ginger said in a cozy, chatty voice. "If I were you, I'd make a list."

"A list?" Eglantine said.

"Yes, a list of all the things that your brother and his friends have left you out of. I think it always makes one feel better to make a list."

Racdrops! Complete racdrops! That idiot owl doesn't even know how to write! Primrose raged silently.

"Hmmm," Eglantine said.

"Making that list will be a relief. Trust me."

Don't trust her! Primrose thought and rushed into the hollow.

"Come on, Eglantine. It's a great night for flying."

"Oh, I don't think we'll be coming Primrose. We have things to do," Ginger said.

Primrose blinked. *All right. I'm finished with being polite.* "I actually didn't ask you, Ginger. I thought with you still healing from your wing injury you wouldn't be up for it, but surely you are Eglantine."

Eglantine looked nervously towards Ginger, almost as if to ask permission to go. "Well... well, maybe just for a little while," Eglantine replied. "But I'll come back early and make that list, don't worry Ginger. Yes, we have important things to do."

"It will be a relief, Eglantine. I promise." Then as Primrose and Eglantine were leaving the hollow to join the others for a few flight frolics under the rising moon, Ginger called out, "A real relief, like sleeping."

Primrose brimmed with joy to be flying with her best friend through the satiny black night. The air was so smooth and soft, soft as an owl chick's down. Ruby, a Short-eared Owl and probably the best flier in the tree, was inscribing figure-of-eights just under the paws of the constellation of the Big Raccoon, which was rising in the eastern sky. Primrose, however, was cautious. She didn't want to get too happy. Things might change. And she certainly didn't want to think about Eglantine making that stupid list. She was wondering if she should say something, not specifically about the list, but about Eglantine feeling left out. She was sure Soren didn't mean to leave her out. He didn't have a choice with this weather experiment thing. And just as she was wondering whether to say something, Eglantine said, "Well, time to get back to the hollow."

"What? Are you yoicks? The night is just beginning. The Big Raccoon is hardly up. I can only see two of his paws."

"Well, look. Soren and the band are taking off to do their weather experiments already."

"That's different. They have things to do. They can't mess around out here like we can. You don't see anyone else taking off for their hollows."

"Well, I have things to do too."

"Like what?" Primrose was flying just beneath Eglantine, and flipped her head backwards and up as only owls can.

"Just things," Eglantine answered vaguely. "And sleep. I want to catch a few winks."

A few winks? That must be an expression she picked up from Ginger. "What do you need to sleep for? Owls don't sleep at night – especially not a night like this."

"Well, I've been feeling kind of tired lately." Eglantine tossed this last comment over her shoulder as she flew off in the direction of the great tree.

Primrose blinked. Maybe there really was something wrong with Eglantine. Maybe she was getting summer flux or grey scale. They said that owls with grey scale slept a lot. *Oh, dear, I hope she isn't really sick.*

CHAPTER FIVE

A fragment from the Sea

Meanwhile, as the Big Raccoon climbed higher and higher in the sky, the band of four – Soren, Twilight, Gylfie and Digger – headed north to a small speck of an island that dripped like the tiniest leak from the peninsula of the Broken Talon. They were flying there to perform their weather experiment for Ezylryb.

The conditions were perfect for setting out the small floats made from bundles of downy feathers and hollowed-out Ga'Hoole nuts.

"Now, what's this all about?" Twilight asked.

"The idea is to measure the wind drift and current variations in this part of the Sea of Hoolemere," Soren replied. "So we set out these little floats, then fly back in a few days and see where they are. Make sure the streamers are well attached because that's how we're going to find them again."

It was fun work, and for a snack when they finished Soren had brought along some barbecued bat wings left over from tweener.

"Glaux, this island is so tiny even I feel big on it," Gylfie said. "Where are we going to light down for a snack?"

"Look over there." Digger flipped his head towards the northern tip of the island. There were three rocks that dribbled off the island, not more than a foot or two away from the shore. "That looks nice enough."

The four owls lighted down on the rocks by a small tide pool. As they ate their bat wings in the moonlight they peered into the shallow water.

"Are starfish good to eat?" Digger asked, spotting one on the bottom.

"They're fish aren't they?" growled Twilight.

"They don't look like fish," Digger said.

"I wouldn't risk it," said Soren. "Remember how that Brown Fish Owl's hollow smelled last autumn in Ambala?"

"Hmmm." Digger looked at the starfish and seemed to think twice about eating it.

"I don't think it would be good for your gizzard," Gylfie said. "I mean bones and fur, that's one thing, but Glaux knows what these creatures are made from. I'd steer clear of it."

"Pretty though, aren't they?" Digger said.

Twilight now bent closer to look at the starfish. "S'pose you could take it back for decoration. They dry out, you know. Might be able to trade it for something with Mags."

"TWILIGHT!" they all shrieked.

"It's alive," Soren said. "You kill things to eat, not for decoration."

"Barely alive, I'd say. Doesn't have a brain, doesn't have a gizzard."

"Still," Gylfie said, "it's alive in its own way."

"S'pose you're right," Twilight said and looked up from his examination of the starfish. "Hey! What's that over there caught in the rocks?"

Something was fluttering between two rocks in the next tide pool. Soren lofted into the air to fly-hop the short distance. "It's a piece of paper." He poked at the piece with his talon. "Or a piece of a piece of paper." And then more slowly, "Or a piece of a page of what was once a book." He blinked at the smeared letters. "Great Glaux... *Fleckasia*! It's part of the book that Dewlap confiscated from Otulissa."

"No!" Gylfie said in a stunned voice.

Soon they were all crowded around Soren and peering at the fragment of the page. Then Digger spoke: "Otulissa will flip her gizzard when she sees this. Can you make out any of the writing? She was just talking about this thing called *shattering*, which fleckasia can cause. It's worse than moon blinking. But she never got to finish the chapter because Dewlap came in and took the book."

"Then Dewlap must have thrown it away," Soren said. "What a complete creep that owl is. Imagine destroying a book like this."

"How did this piece of it ever get this far without completely dissolving?" Gylfie wondered.

"Maybe a seagull picked it up then dropped it here. You know they'll try to eat anything. And it was caught in this little crack where it kept pretty dry," Soren said. "In any case, we have to take this back to Otulissa. Maybe she can make something of it."

When they returned to the great tree, the first pink streaks of dawn were just showing. After a quick breaklight Soren, Digger and Gylfie went to their hollow. Otulissa had completed her experiment for Ezylryb on the far beach but had not yet returned from a special errand for Barran and Boron. She was flying to a slipgizzle who it was thought might have information about the Northern Kingdoms. Soren felt that Boron and Barran were trying to placate Otulissa, who had been plotting a very complex attack on the Pure Ones in which she envisioned enlisting recruits from the Kielian League. Soren and Gylfie had discussed this plan, and both thought it was probably never going to happen. But Boron and Barran seemed to have decided to let Otulissa explore where things stood in the Northern Kingdoms. Ever since Strix Struma had been killed in battle, Otulissa had been obsessed with her plan. In any case, the owls of the band would wait until the next night to show Otulissa the fragment of the page they had found.

In the coolness of the breaking day, the owls nestled into their hollow and, after a few sleepy words, were sound asleep – except for Soren. His mind continued to speculate almost playfully on how that fragment of paper got to where it was between those rocks. He supposed it could have got caught in the sub-Lobelian current. He tried to recall what those current charts looked like and imagine the course that little piece of paper had travelled. He wondered if there were possibly more pieces of paper caught in rocks. No, not a chance, this was a one-in-a-million thing. He yawned again and was asleep.

The sea seemed to float with pieces of paper and oddly enough, the writing on the bits of paper was perfectly legible. But every time Soren swooped down to pick one up, the fog rolled in and he couldn't see. He wished that Twilight were here. Twilight was the master of seeing in conditions like these.

Aaah, finally the fog is lifting. But suddenly, Soren realised that he was no longer over the sea. *Racdrops!* He looked down and saw the regularly undulating hills. *The Beaks!* His gizzard twitched with dread. Mrs Plithiver's raspy voice scratched in his ear: "No owl, especially a young impressionable one, has any business in The Beaks. It's a bad, bad place."

And then below him were the tantalising Mirror Lakes that had transfixed the band in a kind of deadly stupor on their first journey to Ga'Hoole. *Great Glaux.* He blinked at the dazzling sparkle of the lakes beneath him, but those lakes abruptly shattered into thousands of pieces.

"I'm sorry, Mrs Plithiver," he heard himself say. Without even banking, he did a steep dive towards the lakes. He blinked. A dazzling white brightness nearly blinded him. Dread crept around the edges of his gizzard. The radiant brilliance of the shards reminded him of something. Something terrible. What was it? No time to wonder. The fog was drifting back over the lake. Only it wasn't fog. It was smoke – but there was one small clear space above the lake. He would dive for it now. "I'll take these lakes – piece by piece. Yes, Mrs Plithiver, piece by piece by piece."

Soren woke up suddenly and clamped his beak tight. *Great Glaux! It was a dream! I was talking in my sleep!* He looked across at his hollowmates and hoped his babbling hadn't woken them up. But they all seemed to be sleeping peacefully. Soren went back to sleep and would not remember this dream for a long, long time – until it was almost too late!

CHAPTER SIX

So Close!

And in another hollow, another Barn Owl dreamed another dream.

Yes, just like the old fir tree, Eglantine thought. *Just like home. And look, there's moss draped across the opening, the same way Mum did it, to keep out the cold wind, or the sunlight if it was too strong.* She crept closer on the branch. Did she dare peek through? *Why, Great Glaux! Even this branch I am standing on is the same.* Then she heard a soft hiss and a slithering sound. *Why, that's exactly the sound Mrs Plithiver makes when she's tongue-vacuuming and sucking up all the vermin. I'd know that sound anywhere!* Eglantine's gizzard was about to burst with excitement. *This is more than a dream,* she thought. *Oh Glaux, don't let it end! If I peek in, will I see Mum and Da and Mrs P? Will everything be like before?* Eglantine edged in close to the moss curtain. Behind it, she saw a shape bustling about. The whiteness of a Barn Owl's face shone through the green strands of moss. *Is it really you, Mum?* She was about to poke her beak through the curtain and ask. Then a breeze stirred the moss. It riffled through her pinfeathers, a cool current of air. This was no dream about a breeze. She really felt it.

"Wind shift," a voice outside her hollow said. It was Ezylryb.

"Oh no!" moaned Eglantine, and woke up. "I was so close! So close, this time."

"So close?" said Primrose, coming into their hollow. "So close to what? Eglantine, don't tell me you've been sleeping all this time? Glaux, it's not even near morning. How will you ever sleep during the day when we are supposed to?"

Eglantine blinked. "Oh I will." *I have to,* she thought. She was absolutely desperate to get back to her dream hollow.

"Verrry interesting!" Otulissa pored over the fragment that the band had brought back from the island off the Broken Talon peninsula.

"Is it from the book?" Soren asked.

"Definitely," Otulissa replied.

"Can you read it?" Gylfie asked.

"Just barely. There's one word that looks like 'quadrant'."

"Quadrant?" Gylfie said. "That's a navigational term."

"I know," said Otulissa. "I can't imagine why it would show up in a book on fleckasia."

"You know," Soren said, "I've seen Ezylryb fix up old books, especially ones where the pages have faded. He takes Ga'Hoole-nut oil and soaks it into the page. The writing becomes a lot clearer."

"Worth a try." Otulissa looked up. "If only to prove that Dewlap is a traitor and not in the least shattered or having a nervous breakdown."

Soren looked at Gylfie and the same thought went through both their minds. *She's still blaming Dewlap for Strix Struma's death.* Soren wondered if bringing this fragment back had been such a good idea after all. If Otulissa was only using it to get back at Dewlap, it seemed kind of stupid – even wrong – to him. The parliament would never decide to turn her out. It wasn't the Ga'Hoole way. Boron and Barran, the monarchs of the tree, had said as much: *Turn an owl out and it becomes your enemy.* If Dewlap was not a traitor before, she would certainly become one if she were banished.

Instead Dewlap would be relieved of her responsibilities. She would be quietly retired. Already she had been removed from the parliament. That was the supreme dishonour. No owl in the history of the Great Ga'Hoole Tree had ever been removed from the parliament. But Soren knew it was useless to talk to Otulissa about this. She was bound and determined to have her vengeance on Dewlap for the death of her beloved Strix Struma. She had sworn to do so. And she had changed. He had seen that immediately after the last battle of the siege in which Strix Struma had been killed. He had gone to check on Otulissa in her hollow. She was bent over a piece of paper, writing and drawing something. When he had asked what it was, she had said it was an invasion plan. Even though Strix Struma had been killed, the Guardians of Ga'Hoole had won the last battle. Yet somehow the leaders of the so-called Pure Ones, Kludd and his terrifying mate Nyra, whose face shone white as a baleful moon, had escaped. Otulissa's words came back to him:

"They aren't finished with us, Soren. And we can't wait for them to come back and finish."

"What do you mean?" he had asked.

"I mean, Soren, that we can't fight defensively. We have to go after them."

The fury in Otulissa's eyes had made Soren's gizzard roil.

"I've changed," she had said softly. But her voice, Soren remembered, was deadly.

The invasion might wait, but for Otulissa the vengeance was to begin here, right here in the tree, with Dewlap as its target.

A silence fell on the group. They all sensed the pent-up violence in Otulissa, who was normally a reflective, highly intellectual owl. It unnerved them.

"Well," said Gylfie a little too brightly, "isn't it almost time for Trader Mags to arrive? Let's go and wait for her."

"Why would I want any of that ostentatious stuff she's always strutting about with?"

Aaah, that's the old Otulissa, Soren thought thankfully.

"But I guess there's nothing else to do. I'll go," Otulissa said grudgingly.

Madame Plonk, whose ethereal voice sang them to sleep each morning and roused them in the evening with the accompaniment of the grass harp, was as always first in line to survey goods brought in by Trader Mags and her assistant Bubbles, a rather scatterbrained young magpie.

"Oh, Madame Plonk, as gorgeous as ever," Mags addressed the large and lovely Snowy. "What have we here to show off the glorious whiteness of your silken plumage?" Mags cast a sweeping, beady-eyed glance over her goods. "Ah yes. A crimson, ermine-trimmed cape – well, part of a cape."

Trader Mags then swivelled her head towards Primrose, who was examining a drop of amber. "Hold it up to the moonlight, dear. It's got a bug in it. Little, tiny beetle. They say it's a good-luck charm. Not heavy at all. Even a Pygmy like you can fly with it."

"Fool's iron! That's what I call it." Bubo the blacksmith had come up. "But pretty." He nodded towards the amber drop.

It is lovely, Primrose thought. She didn't much believe in good-luck charms, but most of the jewellery and pretty things that Madame Plonk sold were too heavy for a small owl like herself. She had some awfully pretty turquoise chips that she had found in a stream on a search-and-rescue mission once.

"Would you take some turquoise chips for the amber, Trader Mags?" Primrose asked.

"Oh yes, dear. I am mad for turquoise chips. They become me, you know. You have to have a certain plumage and stature for them to show. Run and get your turquoise and I'll wrap up the amber for you."

Soren, who was watching the bargaining from a wingspan away, caught a blur of movement behind a small stand of birch trees where mice could often be found. He decided to explore and, without saying where he was going, slipped away silently.

Soren's beak dropped open in utter horror as he peered down through the slim white branches of the birch tree. Never in his life had he seen anything as revolting as the scene beneath him. An owl had just pounced upon a mouse. After having made a deep gash in its back exposing the spine, the mouse not yet dead but still mewling in agony, the owl had proceeded to tickle the dying creature with a blade of grass, all the while singing a little song. And then, most shocking of all, Soren recognised his own sister, Eglantine, who seemed frozen in rapt attention, watching as her friend Ginger sang, tickling and playing with what she would soon eat. This was in violation of every food and hunting law in the owl kingdom. Where had this Barn Owl been raised? What kind of family allowed this sort of behaviour? Without thinking, Soren swooped down and thwacked the mouse on the head, killing it instantly, and then gulped it down headfirst in proper fashion.

"Hey, no fair! Why did you do that? That was my mouse."

Soren glared at Ginger. "You are a disgrace to the tree, a disgrace to every owl kingdom on the face of the earth. What sort of creature plays with her food? You don't deserve to eat." Then he swivelled his head towards Eglantine. "Eglantine, you go back to my hollow. I'll talk to you there." Eglantine blinked. It was as if she were coming out of a spell.

"You're always ordering her around. She doesn't like it. And you never include her. She feels left out," Ginger said.

"I hope she feels left out of this!" Soren *shree*d, in the high-pitched tone of voice understood instantly by all owls to express anger. "Eglantine, on your way. And you!" He turned his attention back to Ginger. "You, I am reporting to Boron and Barran."

"Oh Soren, don't report her. She's been raised by those awful owls, the Pure Ones. They never taught her anything. They were brutes, all of them," Eglantine pleaded. Within seconds both Ginger and Eglantine were sobbing.

"She's right. I know nothing," Ginger was saying, suddenly contrite. "I learned nothing except bad manners."

"This is beyond bad manners. This is brutality."

"Well yeah. That too," she replied. "Your own brother was the most brutal owl imaginable."

"Yes, but I'm not, and Eglantine's not. And we were all born in the same tree, in the same hollow, in the same nest to the same parents. We are not like Kludd, and you don't have to be this way either. Don't use excuses. You're among civilised owls now. Haven't you learned anything?"

"Oh yes, so much. So much from your sister."

Soren saw that Eglantine was yawning now. When Soren had mentioned the tree, the hollow, the nest and their parents, it had made her think of her dream.

"What are you yawning about, Eglantine? You're always yawning. Don't you get enough sleep?"

"No, I don't think she does," Ginger said. "I think she might have summer flux."

"Oh great. Now you're a doctor?"

"Just don't report her, Soren. Please!" Eglantine yawned again, and her eyes fluttered as if she could barely keep them open.

"All right, all right. But Eglantine, I want you to sleep in my hollow. Then you'll feel included, right?"

"Right," Eglantine said sleepily.

"But what about me?" whined Ginger.

"What about you?" Soren shot back.

"I'm not included. Now I feel left out."

"Tough pellets! When you learn not to play with your food, maybe you'll be fit to be included."

Soren made sure that Eglantine was bedded down in his hollow and then went to find Gylfie. "You're not going to believe what I just saw."

"Look over there," Gylfie replied, nodding in the direction of Trader Mags. "Do you believe what you're seeing now?"

Otulissa was oohing and aahing over some stick that Trader Mags had. "You really have the most enormously interesting collection. Let me see. What can I trade you for this stick? And look, after giving you all my finest lucky stones for that chart, I almost don't have any left over. You really are wonderful."

Soren could not believe his exceptionally good ears. "Stick? Chart? Trader Mags is 'wonderful'?" What had happened to the Otulissa who had never approved of the magpie trader?

"She's struck gold with Trader Mags," Gylfie whispered excitedly. "That stick is a dowsing rod for finding flecks in the ground or in streams. The chart is a diagram of the owl brain, cross-referenced to a diagram of the gizzard, which could help explain fleckasia."

"Glaux! I guess she did strike gold," Soren replied.

CHAPTER SEVEN

The Sign of the Centipede

"I can't believe we're going to find any flecks around here," Gylfie said.

The band was walking behind Otulissa through a grove of trees on the southern side of the island as she stepped carefully with the divining rod in her beak. She was quite awkward with it and often dropped it.

"Can you imagine what that stick would do in the canyons of St Aggie's?" Twilight said.

"Shake itself to bits," Digger replied. "Otulissa, why don't you let an experienced walker like myself try that thing?" The Spotted Owl had dropped the stick again.

"All right, my beak is tired from holding it."

Digger picked up the rod and walked in graceful strides while swinging his head in arcs.

It was getting a little boring. The rod had not given the slightest quiver. But for Soren it was a nice break from worrying about Eglantine. It was decided that she was suffering from some form of summer flux. She had been put in the infirmary where all she did was sleep and dream some pleasant dream that she was always anxious to get back to. Recently though, the infirmary matron had reported that she was sleeping somewhat less. She had even roused herself the previous evening to go out on a short flight with Primrose and Ginger.

The night was now getting old however, and soon it would be time to return to the tree for breaklight and then sleep. So the owls decided to put the rod aside and go out for a quick flight over the moonlit Sea of Hoolemere. It was a beautiful summer evening and there promised to be plenty of scooters, for the day had been quite hot. Scooters were land breezes that spilled off the edge of the cooling island. Because land cooled faster than water, it created silky winds that could be ridden almost without stirring one's wings. They were great fun to play in and the owls could slide down their gentle slopes until almost hitting the water. They had been doing this for several minutes when Gylfie spotted Eglantine and Ginger.

"Look Soren, there's your sister, up and about!"

"Oh good! She must be feeling better." He climbed up the wind slope and when he reached the top called out, "Eglantine! Ginger!" He was trying extra hard to be nice to Ginger. He felt that Eglantine had been right in a way – Ginger, after all, had known only the brutal ways of the Pure Ones and her bad behaviour really wasn't all her fault. And Ginger did seem to respond well to his kindness. She seemed much nicer and was genuinely trying to learn the ways of civilised owls. The three of them now sought a perch in a spruce tree that somehow clung to the rocky edge above the beach.

"Where have you two been?"

"Halfway across the sea!" Eglantine exclaimed with delight. "I think I really am getting better. I'm not sleeping nearly as much. I think it's that tonic matron has been giving me."

"And she's getting stronger too," Ginger added.

But what Eglantine did not tell anyone was that although she wasn't sleeping as much, her dreams had become even more intense. And more important, she now knew they were not just dreams but were real and true. Out there – somewhere – was a hollow just like the one in which she and Soren had been hatched, and their mother was there waiting for them. It wasn't in the Forest of Tyto but rather, she suspected, in the region known as The Beaks. She could see this place perfectly in her dream. The hollow was in a fir tree and it was near a beautiful shining lake. She hadn't told anybody yet, not even Primrose or Ginger. But she knew if she stayed awake a little longer each night and tried to fly as hard as she could, soon she would be strong enough to fly there.

And then what joy there would be! She would be Soren's hero. She would be the one who found their parents. And Soren would never again dare leave her out of anything. They would all be happy together. Eglantine had already figured out that they would live together here in the Great Ga'Hoole Tree part of the year and then the other part of the year in their own private hollow in The Beaks, or maybe even back in Tyto. And Mrs Plithiver would come along and keep everything as neat and perfect as she had before. Yes, it would all be so perfect, and she just knew that her parents were so smart that Boron and Barran would ask them to be rybs. Oh it would all be so wonderful.

Eglantine and Ginger flew back to the tree with the other owls who had been out. They headed towards Mrs P's table for breaklight.

"Good news!" Mrs P said as they gathered around her for one of their favourite summer meals, milkberry jelly with a small bug set right in the middle.

"What's that?" said Soren.

"Matron says that Eglantine is well enough to return to her own hollow to sleep."

"You were out flying tonight," Gylfie said to Eglantine. "So you must be feeling a lot better."

"Yes," Eglantine said.

"Oh great!" Primrose said. She had missed Eglantine so much when she was gone. But she had to admit that Ginger was a lot nicer than she had been at first.

"But," Mrs P continued, "you have to keep taking the tonic, Eglantine."

"Oh, I will. I promise."

"Oh," Primrose exclaimed. "I got a dragonfly in my jelly. My favourite!"

The other owls began poking at their milkberry jelly to see what bug might be embedded in the lilac-coloured treat.

Eglantine peered down into her own jelly. It wasn't a slug or a grasshopper. It was a centipede, her very favourite bug. It had to be a sign – a sign that her dreams were real. Her mum had always brought back centipedes as a special treat for her, and Soren would sing the centipede song. She looked up at Soren now with huge, blinking eyes.

"Eglantine, you're not going to make me sing the centipede song here?" he whispered.

Eglantine giggled. "No, don't worry." And she might have said aloud what she was thinking: *I don't need the centipede song to prove that my dream is real. Mum is waiting for me with a dozen centipedes, I just know it!*

The shortest night and longest day of the year were approaching. It was called Nimsy night and all of the owls looked forward to it because it was after Nimsy that the nights began to grow longer by slivers, first in seconds, then in minutes and finally, at summer's end, by hours. Eglantine had decided that she would fly to the hollow in The Beaks after Nimsy, when the longer nights would give her more time.

However, on these short summer nights and long summer days before Nimsy, the owls tended to stay up longer and go to sleep later. There were only so many hours an owl could sleep during the day, especially when their night flight exercise was cut short.

"Let's go to the library," Otulissa said. "I want to study this chart."

On one of the larger tables, Otulissa unrolled the chart she had got from Trader Mags. It showed a diagram of the owl brain cross-referenced with a diagram of the owl gizzard. *Perhaps it could help explain fleckasia*, Otulissa thought. "If I only had that whole book on fleckasia," she sighed.

"But you have that page we found when we were out doing weather experiments for Ezylryb," Gylfie said.

"Yes, but it was hardly legible." Otulissa stared down at the diagram. "Quadrant!" she suddenly said in a hushed voice. With a shaking talon, Otulissa pointed to the chart.

"You see the word 'quadrant' in both that section of the brain and that section of the gizzard. The very word that was on the torn page you found! I'll be back in a second." Otulissa flapped her wings and flew out of the library. In less than a minute she was back with the torn page in her beak. She bent over the page and peered. Then swung her head towards the chart. "There's the number two, look. I can barely make it out but it's there." She blinked and slowly began to speak. "I get it. See. The gizzard is divided into four quadrants and so is the brain."

"And so is the night sky for navigation," Gylfie said. "Strix Struma taught us that."

"Right!" Otulissa said. "When Ezylryb was lost, it was because the bags of flecks had destroyed his sense of the quadrants for navigation. He no longer knew where the earth's magnetic poles were."

A creaky voice scratched the air. "Indeed, Otulissa. You are right." It was Ezylryb. "Aha! A humours chart," the old Whiskered Screech proclaimed.

"Humours?" Twilight said. "What's so funny about an owl gizzard and brain?"

"It's not *ha-ha* humour. No, not in the least. The lost book, *Fleckasia and Other Disorders of the Gizzard*, would have explained much about humours… and how they relate to shattering."

Soren blinked. Shattering was the terrible disease that Otulissa had told them about.

"Tell me, Ezylryb," Soren asked hesitantly. "Is that what's wrong with Dewlap? Was she shattered?"

Ezylryb sighed heavily then shook his head. "No, she is not shattered. She is an old and foolish owl. Still, there was no rupture between the gizzard and brain. She was just misguided, used bad judgement and her focus was limited. She felt the Pure Ones would take better care of the tree than we would."

"But what exactly is 'shattering'?" Otulissa asked.

"It is very complicated, Otulissa. It is even beyond higher magnetics, which I know you know a lot about. But without the book, I don't know how I could begin to explain it."

"It's connected to higher magnetics?" Otulissa asked.

"Oh, indeed it is. You know how in all of our brains there are tiny bits of magnetic particles much smaller than flecks. They are sometimes called iron oxides. They aid us with navigation because they help us sense the earth's magnetic field."

Primrose had come into the library and was now also listening intently.

"Imagine, however, if something disturbed those bits in our brain," Ezylryb continued. "Exposure to too many flecks not only causes problems to the internal compass that we use for navigational purposes, as it did mine, but in certain conditions it can cause a shattering to other vital systems. In fact, sometimes it is not the navigational system that is affected but the gizzard. The gizzard itself becomes almost like stone, incapable of sorting out feelings and emotions. It can even cause delusions. That is what fleckasia is all about."

"Well, is there a book on the humours or these quadrants, so I can find out more?" Otulissa asked.

"Oh, yes indeed. Here, let me show you." Ezylryb made his way towards a far shelf in the library, and Otulissa bustled behind him. The other four owls looked at one another. This was Otulissa's kind of thing, not theirs. Soren was thankful that Ezylryb had come in. Perhaps if Otulissa began sinking herself into a study of fleckasia, she would ease up on her battle plans for attacking the Pure Ones. She was sure they would be back. She kept saying, "First strike! We must make the first strike!" But Soren knew she would never convince Boron and Barran or any of the parliament members. It was absolutely against the tradition of the Guardians to strike the first blow, certainly not on the scale that Otulissa was planning.

"Can I come and look at the book, too?" Primrose asked.

Otulissa blinked as did the others. Primrose had never struck them as much of an intellect. "Sure," said Otulissa.

"Just want to take a peek," Primrose said.

The sun was well up over the horizon by the time the owls made their way to their hollows. Eglantine was tired because that night had been the first long-distance flight she had made in some time. Madame

Plonk had begun to sing the "Night Is Done" song, and by the time she reached the second verse Eglantine was sound asleep.

Primrose had come back to the hollow she shared with Ginger and Eglantine just after Madame Plonk had begun the song. She had been reading with Otulissa in the library the whole time. Now, as she entered the hollow, Ginger woke up.

"Where've you been?"

"Reading in the library," Primrose answered.

"Must have been interesting."

For the second time ever, Primrose lied outright. "Oh, just doing some of those game and riddle books that Eglantine loves so much." She looked over and blinked at her best friend. Then she turned again to Ginger and whispered, "I do hope she stops having those dreams. I know she says they are lovely but I think they're not. She twitches all night long when she has them."

"Yes," said Ginger sleepily. "I know what you mean. Sometimes I just get up and pat her, and it seems to calm her down a little."

"That's kind of you, Ginger," Primrose said. *I really must be nicer to this owl*, she thought. *She's not so bad. And soon it will be Nimsy night. Everyone always feels better once the earth turns and chases away the sun and lets the nights grow longer.* She listened to the end of the beautiful song. The lovely *ting* of Madame Plonk's voice now hung like silver chimes in the morning as she sang the next verse.

We thank thee for our nights
'Neath the moon and stars so bright
We are home in our tree
We are owls, we are free
As we go, this we know, Glaux is nigh.

Soon Primrose was asleep. Late in the afternoon she heard a stirring and sleepily opened one eye. Ginger was bent over Eglantine. *Oh dear. She must be having one of those dreams and Ginger is patting her.* Then Primrose yawned and sank back into sleep.

Eglantine was having a dream. She had finally poked her beak through the strands of moss. From behind, the female owl looked exactly like her mother. She was about to say "Mum" when the owl turned around. She did look like her mum! Almost, but not quite. Her face seemed whiter and there was a seam across it where the feathers parted a bit.

"I've been waiting for you all this time!"

"You have?!"

"Yes, darling one!"

Something seemed to jolt Eglantine in her sleep. *Darling.* That word sounded odd coming from her mum. It wasn't a word she used. But still she was drawn in.

"Who are you?"

"Why, you know who I am! And no need to wait until so long after Nimsy night. You'll be ready much sooner, darling..."

The jolt coursed through her again. And then her eyes blinked open. The soft lavender of twilight had seeped into the hollow. She looked over at Primrose's corner. The Pygmy Owl was already up and out of the hollow, but Ginger was still sleeping. The dream Eglantine had just experienced was more real than ever. Her mum had said that she would be ready soon! Ready to go soon after Nimsy night. This was so exciting. Oh, she just had to tell someone. She looked over at Ginger again. She was beginning to stir. What would Ginger say if she told her about the dream? Would she think that she was just plain yoicks? Ginger's eyes blinked open now and Eglantine hopped over to where she slept.

"Ginger, I have to tell you something." The Barn Owl was instantly alert. "Promise you won't think I've gone yoicks."

"Why would I ever think that? You are one of the most sensible owls I have ever met," Ginger replied.

"Promise on your gizzard not to tell?"

Ginger touched the feathers on her belly and said, "On my gizzard. Now, what is it?"

"All right." Eglantine took a deep breath. "Well, I have been having these dreams, you know."

Ginger nodded.

"And, well, I think they are actually more than just dreams. They are very real in a way. They are telling me something."

"What are they telling you, Eglantine?" Ginger said in a very soft voice.

"My mum is alive, and I think my da is too. And I think I know where they are." She paused. "The Beaks."

"I believe you, Eglantine. Why wouldn't I believe you? They say that your brother Soren has starsight. Why shouldn't you too dream about things before they happen?"

"You're right! Ginger, I never thought of that. It must run in the family. Oh my goodness. I am so glad I told you. And you know what else?"

"No, what?" Ginger said eagerly.

"Well, I just know I can find that hollow in The Beaks and my mum wants me to come. I had already decided to go maybe a month or so after Nimsy night because the darkness will hold longer then, and I would have more time to get there. But mum, I mean my dream mum, says that I'll be ready before that. She says I'll soon be strong enough for the flight."

"Oh, that's wonderful, and of course, who knows you better than your own mum? Mums know best."

Eglantine blinked. *How does Ginger always know exactly the right thing to say?* Eglantine thought. Ginger was the most wonderful hollowmate.

CHAPTER EIGHT

Mum Waits for Me

Nimsy night had come and gone and as the day's light dissolved minute by minute earlier and earlier, and the nights grew longer, the owls of the Great Ga'Hoole Tree grew happier because night was indeed their element. The long hot days pressed thickly upon them as they slept, the time passing so slowly, creeping by at the pace of a sluggish caterpillar until the cool of the evening descended and the sky turned faintly lavender, then deep purple and finally black. For Eglantine, each extra minute of the black was a cause for celebration. She flew now with great enthusiasm and growing strength in each class – whether it was her own chaw practice for search-and-rescue with the lovely

Burrowing Owl Sylvanaryb, or navigation class, now under the leadership of a Barred Owl named Woody, who had succeeded the late Strix Struma as the navigation ryb.

Soren was pleased to see Eglantine acting like her old self and free of the summer flux or whatever the strange sleeping sickness was that had afflicted her earlier. Indeed, everyone except Primrose seemed pleased with Eglantine's recovery. But Primrose was not sure. Yes, Eglantine seemed better, but she knew that she still twitched while she dreamed. Often she would awake sleepily to see Ginger bent over her. And yes, it was true that now the three of them, Ginger, Primrose and Eglantine, did many things together, so she could not accuse Eglantine of leaving her out.

Still, Primrose sensed that there was a bond between Eglantine and Ginger – an inviolable bond. There was something they shared and Primrose was not sure what it was. Some things shared are good, but others are not. Some secrets that are shared strengthen one, but others can sap one's strength in insidious ways. Primrose thought this might be happening with Eglantine, who seemed to be growing stronger in flight after her weeks of languishing in sleep. Yes, her wings were back to full power, but something else was growing weaker by the minute. Primrose sensed it.

Now, almost a week after Nimsy night, Eglantine and Ginger seemed especially excited. Although they were never so impolite as to whisper to each other in the dining hollow as they had once done, Primrose would find them huddled together on limbs of the Ga'Hoole Tree, and as soon as she would light down, they would clamp their beaks shut and be almost too nice to her. She also noticed that on free flights, when there were no classes, Ginger and Eglantine would often just slip away.

So it was after seeing the two young owls slip off three nights in a row that Primrose decided that one night soon she would follow them. She was sure they were up to something. She was turning all this over in her mind at tweener.

"You got the slug, Primrose!" Soren exclaimed.

The slug was the best thing to find in one's jelly. It meant an extra helping of dessert.

"I did!"

"Great Glaux, if I hadn't pointed it out you would never have noticed."

Primrose blinked. Soren was right. She had been so absorbed in her thoughts she had nearly missed the slug. She ate it quickly then blinked once, twice, and then a huge belch issued from her beak. She keeled over right on top of Mrs Plithiver.

"Oh dear!" Mrs P said. "Is that Primrose?"

A great commotion followed.

"Bad slug! Bad slug!" someone yelled. "Call the matrons!"

Eglantine looked stunned and fearful as they carried Primrose out. "Is she going to be all right?" she cried desperately.

"Just a bad slug, dear," Barran said. "Don't worry about it. She'll be all right. They'll give her a glister and that will fix her up just fine. Weak for a couple of days. It is a harsh treatment. But she'll recover. We must have a talk with Cook about being more careful with the slugs."

"Guess she won't have her second helping," Ginger said. "Who gets it?"

Soren and Digger both turned their gaze on her and blinked.

Then Otulissa spoke. "You know, that really frinks me off, Ginger."

They all felt Mrs Plithiver flinch at the sound of the swear word. Otulissa turned and glared at Ginger. "I hardly think this is a moment to celebrate. Perhaps Primrose can have it when she recovers. In fact, I think she should get two extra helpings."

"Just asking," Ginger said in a small voice.

"Well don't," Gylfie replied tartly.

"Sorry," Ginger muttered.

"What's wrong, Ginger?" Eglantine asked after tweener and before free flight that evening.

"Nobody likes me here. I do everything wrong. They are all still mad at me for asking about the extra helping, even after I said I was sorry."

"That's not true, Ginger. The owls like you. They understand that you've been brought up differently."

"Yeah, and they never let me forget it. I bet your mum wouldn't be that way. I bet she'd accept me just the way I am."

"You're probably right." Eglantine nodded and a dreamy look filled her eyes.

But then it seemed as if a wary silence hung between them, as if neither one of them dared to say what they were thinking.

Wouldn't it be lovely, Eglantine thought, *if Ginger could come and stay with us. Mum would love her. I just know it. I'd have a sister at last.*

Finally, the silence was broken by Ginger. She had swivelled her head and was looking out the hollow's opening. "Look. The wind has shifted. It's blowing from the north, right towards The Beaks. They call it a sweet wind, don't they?"

"Yes, it's a sweet wind if it blows towards the southeast in the summer. I'm not sure why. Maybe it cools things down in the worst of the summer heat. *But it's a sign*, Eglantine thought. *Yes, the sweet wind is a sign just as the centipede in the milkberry jelly was a sign that Mum is near, and I should go to her. The sweet wind will carry me there.*

"Ginger, I have an idea."

"Yes?" Ginger leaned forward eagerly, her dark eyes shining.

"I think with this favourable wind, this sweet wind, I could easily make it to my mum's hollow in The Beaks tonight."

"I think you could too, Eglantine," she said. Then she cast her eyes down shyly. Eglantine could tell that Ginger wanted to say something more, but for some reason she was having trouble getting the words out.

"What is it, Ginger?"

"I'm not sure I can ask this. It seems so... so... I don't know."

"Ginger, do you want to know if you can come with me? Is that it?"

Ginger gave a barely discernible nod and then fluttered her eyelids.

"Why, of course you can. I wouldn't think of going without you. Mum will love you."

"Really?"

"Really," replied Eglantine. "Now, when should we go?"

"I think we should leave as soon as free flight begins tonight. There are no classes all night, and I bet every owl will be over on the north side of the island riding those northerly wind crests as they come in."

"You're right. It's been so hot. They'll all be over there cooling off in those chilly crests."

"But we can pick up the sweet wind on the south side. No one will know where we've gone. They'll just think we're off doing something else."

"I hope so," Eglantine said in a tentative voice. She was thinking how she had just been complaining yesterday to Soren, and he had said that they might get the northerly wind soon. But if she and Ginger left right now they could pretend that they had flown off before they knew the wind crests were arriving. Yes, that was what they must do! Eglantine was so thrilled at the prospect of seeing her mum that she thought her gizzard might just burst from the joy.

At last I am going towards something, I'm going home! Home! To Mum, to Da perhaps, to our family hollow. As the two Barn Owls circled out and climbed over the Sea of Hoolemere, the moon rose and cast a glinting silver thread of light that led right to The

Beaks. For Eglantine, it seemed as if she had lived in an empty hollow forever; yes, that was what death meant for those who had not died but grieved endlessly. The grieving life was a large bare hollow, with long empty flight paths leading to it. But now she knew everything was about to change. Her life would have meaning again. With her mum and da, she was somebody and she would live in a lovely mossy hollow hung with vines of ivy and lichen, listening to their stories. Their legends of that place called the Great Ga'Hoole Tree. To them, it was just a legend. Eglantine knew the tree was real, but it didn't really count, not like a hollow, not like home.

She began to hum a song that she had often heard her mother sing. Oh, she wished she could remember the words. Her mother had sung it when she was returning to the nest from hunting. It was halfway between a hunting song and a lullaby. Suddenly, the words came back to her and Eglantine began singing the lovely old song.

I'm coming home to my tall tree
In a forest deep and green,
Where my owl chicks wait for me
Tucked away in my tall tree.
I bring you vole,

I bring coon.
The blood's not cold,
I'll be there soon.
And from my breast,
I'll pluck some down,
So you can rest
'Til the moon grows round.
Sleep on, babes, grow strong.
May your feathers fledge,
Your wings grow long.
And then at day's edge
When dark drinks light,
We'll rise together in chick's first flight.

Like a seam in the night, the coastline of The Beaks began to glimmer.

"This way," Eglantine cried out to Ginger and tipped her head towards a lake that was shining in the distance. It sparkled with the reflections of the moon and the stars. Eglantine had never seen anything so beautiful. "It's like a mirror!" she exclaimed, and when she looked down she could see both of their faces.

"But look over there, Eglantine – a tree, a fir tree! Just like the one you told me about. The one in your dreams!"

"But this isn't a dream, Ginger. This is REAL!"

And she swooped out across the lake, heading straight towards the fir tree. And she began singing once more.

I'm coming home to my tall tree
In a forest deep and green,
Where my mum waits for me
Tucked away in my tall tree.
Oh, my mum waits for me!

CHAPTER NINE

The Most Beautiful Mum in the World

Eglantine lighted down on the branch. She cocked her head towards the opening of the hollow. Was she really hearing the same song she had just been singing? And in her mum's voice? She took a couple of steps tentatively towards the opening.

"Look, she's braided the moss, Ginger, just like she always did in Tyto."

"Go on in. Don't be bashful," Ginger urged. "It's your mum, for Glaux's sake."

"What if she doesn't recognise me? I was just a baby then."

"A mother always knows her own chick, even when that chick has grown up and fledged flight feathers."

Trembling, Eglantine crept closer to the opening. Then with one talon, she very shyly began to part some of the moss strands. Her mum's back was to her. It looked as if she was plucking some down from her own breast and arranging it in a soft bed. There must be eggs in there, chicks on the way. *There won't be room for me!* she thought and started to back away. At that moment, the owl turned round.

"Who's there?" she said. A breath seemed to lock in Eglantine's throat. Her gizzard quaked. It wasn't a scroom. It was her mum... almost. Something was a tiny bit different. Eglantine felt a shove from behind her. It was Ginger firmly pushing her through the moss curtain.

"Eglantine?" It sounded like her mother. "Eglantine," the owl repeated again. "Mercy, it's really you."

She looked almost exactly like her mum, but Eglantine hadn't remembered her mum's face as looking so white or so large. It was almost as if the moon had floated into this hollow. And there was a line that ran diagonally across her face where the feathers had grown back not as thickly as before so there was a bit of pink showing through. But in truth, her mother had never looked so beautiful, scar or no scar. This was one of the most beautiful Barn Owls Eglantine had ever seen. She seemed larger than her mother. But her voice was identical.

"Come in, darling. Come in."

Eglantine blinked hard. "Why'd you call me darling? You never called me that before."

A small shudder passed through the owl. "Well... uh... it's been so long. I can't remember everything. But I do remember that your favourite bug is a centipede, and look what I have here for you right beside your nest."

She moved to one side. It wasn't a nest with new eggs in it. No, it was a little berth for Eglantine, fixed up just the way her mum had always done it, with layers of moss, then down from her own breast, then more moss, then more down, and beside it a little pile of centipedes.

"Oh Mum," Eglantine cried, and rushed to her mother's breast.

Her mum's huge wings wrapped around her. And then while still holding her close, her mum picked up a dried centipede with one talon and began to sing. She sang in a small childish voice that sounded quite strange. It was an old song from Eglantine's earliest chick days, when she ate only insects.

What gives a wriggle
And makes you giggle
When you eat 'em?
Whose weensy little feet
Make my heart really beat?
Why, it's those little creepy crawlies
That make me feel so jolly
For the darling centipede –
My favourite buggy feed.
I always want some more,
That's the insect I adore.
More than beetles, more than crickets,
Which at times give me the hiccups,
I crave only to feed
On a juicy centipede
And I shall be happy for evermore.

Eglantine pushed herself away a bit from her mother. "Mum, you remember the song."

"Of course, my darl— I mean dear. Didn't I hear Soren sing it to you enough times?"

"Yes… yes…" Eglantine said hesitantly. She looked more closely at her mother. Something seemed just a little bit off.

"Mum, your face seems so big and so white."

"Well, we do all change a bit, dearest."

Mum sometimes called me dearest. But it was usually dearest Eggie. She's sort of got it by half. But never darling. Her mum's explanation made Eglantine feel a bit more comfortable. But she felt that she was not quite as happy, quite as relieved as she should be.

"But what's that line down your face?"

"Just a scratch, dear. A silly little collision during a storm with a flying branch. That's all."

"But where's Da?"

"Out hunting with Kludd and Soren."

"But that can't be."

"Well, why ever not?"

"Soren's at the great tree, the Great Ga'Hoole Tree."

"Now Eglantine. We don't tell fibs."

"It's not a fib, Mum. It's a real place."

"It's a legend, dearest, that's all. And when your da gets back, he'll tell you stories of it as he always does before you go to sleep."

"But I don't think I can stay here all through the day. I'll be missed."

"Who could ever miss you more than me, your own mother?"

Eglantine was getting more confused by the second. She looked around for Ginger. "I brought a friend. Where is she?"

"Well, there was no one here but you, darling."

"No, Ginger was here. I'm sure she came with me. I told her that she could stay with us. She's an orphan."

"Oh dear, how sad." Her mother sighed. "Of course, darl— dearest. We always have room for another."

"I knew you'd feel that way, Mum. I told her she would be welcome." Eglantine said all this while studying her mother as if she were trying to convince herself of some truth. "I just don't know where she could have gone to now."

"Well, perhaps she wanted to leave the two of us alone. You know, so we could be just mother and daughter. It's been so long."

"Yes it has," Eglantine said in barely a whisper.

"But I'm going to feed you all your favourite things – centipedes and a nice plump vole and a bit of field mouse."

"Oh yum!" Eglantine said, for she suddenly discovered that she was ravenously hungry.

She ate, yawned, and wondered vaguely where Ginger could have gone. Then, just before she fell asleep in a nest especially prepared by her mother with the loveliest mosses and her mum's own down plucked from her very own breast, Eglantine did manage to say in a slow, groggy voice, "Mum, please don't let me sleep too long. I will be in trouble if I don't get back in time. It may be a legend to you, but it's something real to me."

"Of course, darling. It's all too real for many." And just as Eglantine's eyes shut, there was a flash of harsh light that slid into the hollow like the edge of the sharpest blade.

On a limb outside the hollow a huge Barn Owl perched as the moonlight struck his metal mask.

CHAPTER TEN

Eglantine Researches

Am I here? Am I there? In her dream she had felt the softest moss and fluffiest down, but something was a bit more scratchy now, not like the softness of the nest she had dreamed of. Eglantine's eyes blinked open. It was full daylight. There was Ginger. They were back in their hollow at the Great Ga'Hoole Tree. She knew she had been somewhere, to the dream hollow, but she had not gone there in a dream. *I really went there. I think I saw Mum. She said "Come back," but how in the world did I get back here?*

Eglantine had no recollection of flying back. She looked around the hollow. Where was Primrose? *Oh yes, in the infirmary,* she remembered. And she had promised to go and visit her at tween time when everyone would be getting up. She resettled herself in what she now felt to be an exceedingly scratchy bed of moss with no nice fluffy down, and she waited for sleep to come.

But sleep didn't come. In fact, Eglantine was not at all sleepy. She felt wide awake and had a sudden urge to go to the library. She got up and flew from the hollow, weaving through the bright sunlight of midday, spiralling upwards in the tree towards the entrance to the library. Nobody would be there now. It would be empty. Not even Ezylryb – who was always in the library – ever came at this time of the day.

Normally Eglantine went to the shelf with the game books and puzzles, but for some reason these seemed boring to her now. So instead she went to another shelf, the shelf that Otulissa loved, the one that had the books on higher magnetics and flecks. Great Glaux, she remembered the fuss about these books last winter when Dewlap had wanted them declared spronk, or forbidden, which of course was absolutely opposed to everything the Guardians of Ga'Hoole stood for. They believed that no knowledge should ever be forbidden.

And how right they were, Eglantine suddenly thought. *All of this should be shared! It's my duty! My mission!*

And so she plucked a book from the shelf with the title of *Higher Magnetics: The Destructive Powers* and began to read. *Great Glaux, this is fascinating!* She wondered why she had ever wasted her time on game books. She was worried she might not remember it all, so she went and fetched a paper, quill and ink so she could make a few notes.

She had been working several hours before she realised that the harsh light of noon had begun to leak out of the library hollow from its opening and a softer light began to slip in. Although she did not feel at all tired, for some reason she did not want to be discovered in the library even though it was approaching a more normal hour for such study. She rolled up her papers and decided to go back to her own hollow and catch a nap. It would be at least another hour until Madame Plonk sang "Day Is Done, Night Has Come" to rouse them. There was one other thing she had wanted to do. What was it? Oh yes. Primrose. She had wanted to go and see Primrose in the infirmary. Oh well, there would be time for that later.

When she returned to her hollow, Eglantine saw that Ginger was still sleeping. She tucked her papers into a small niche and settled down. It seemed as if she had only been asleep five minutes when the first chords from the grass harp threaded through the twilight and Madame Plonk's voice shimmered with the "Day Is Done" song and woke her up.

Now twilight came and Ginger roused herself. Eglantine simply had to ask her if the trip to The Beaks had really happened and how they had got back.

"Ginger," she said slowly. "We were there, weren't we?"

"Where?"

"You know where. At my mum's in The Beaks."

"Yes. We flew there," Ginger assured her. "Don't you remember?"

"Sort of, but I have no memory of coming back."

"Well you did. Here you are."

"But where were you?"

"Where was I when?" Ginger asked.

"You seemed to disappear when I went into the hollow with Mum."

"Eglantine, I was there the whole time. Maybe you were just so excited about seeing your mum you didn't notice. But I was there. I heard your mum sing that cute little centipede song."

"You did?" Eglantine asked, genuinely excited. *That means it really happened. Mum is alive.*

"I did. Your mum was so nice to me."

"She was?"

"She certainly was," Ginger answered.

"Oh, I can't wait to go back. Do you think we can slip away again tonight?"

"I don't see why not."

"I wonder if I should tell Soren."

"Oh, I wouldn't rush that," Ginger said. "Don't you want to have your mum all to yourself for a while?"

"Well," Eglantine hesitated.

"Look. You've been left out so much," Ginger said soothingly, "you should have something that's just for you."

"Yes, yes, I suppose you're right." For a sliver of a second Eglantine felt a tiny bit greedy, but she quickly forgot about the feeling and basked in the anticipation of her mum's love and attention.

So night after summer night, Eglantine and Ginger managed to slip away. Certain odd things happened to Eglantine's mind and her memory on these visits. She could never, for instance, quite recall how she got back from The Beaks, and it seemed odd to her that Ginger was rarely in her mum's hollow. And her father never appeared. But none of this bothered her much, just as her mum's occasional slips of calling her 'darling' stopped bothering her. She quickly forgot about anything disturbing, just as she had forgotten to tell Soren about having found their mother, and just as she had forgotten about visiting Primrose in the infirmary. No, once she flew over The Beaks and neared the hollow, all her concerns and worries simply melted away.

And her mum was always so proud of her, especially her reading and her writing skills. Her mum saved every little paper Eglantine brought her and praised her fine penmanship. She always showed such interest in the books that Eglantine was reading.

"There's one, Mum, that tells all about flecks and how to make more flecks from flecks." At this her mum grew very excited.

"Oh darling! I would love to know about that. Please copy that one down."

"Oh Mum, I don't know. It's in a very big book with a lot of writing on each page and very complicated diagrams."

"Well, darling, I think if you would just tear out a couple of the pages, no one would notice."

Eglantine blinked. Did something perhaps prick at the back of her mind? Did her gizzard perhaps flinch ever so slightly? No, it hardly stirred at all any more. She simply said, "Sure, I'll get it next time."

And she did.

CHAPTER ELEVEN

Primrose's Last Thought

"But Eglantine, I was in the infirmary for two weeks and never once did you come to visit me. Not one time." Primrose peered at her friend in genuine confusion.

Eglantine blinked. "I'm sorry, it just slipped my mind." But she didn't look the least bit sorry. She did look different though. Her usually lustrous black eyes had a dull gaze to them. Primrose didn't know what to think. "I've been so busy, you know."

"No, I don't know," Primrose replied. "How would I if you never came to visit me?"

"Oh well. I've been busy, trust me."

And it was when Eglantine said those two simple words 'trust me' that something clicked in Primrose's brain and her gizzard gave a painful little twitch. Primrose did not trust Eglantine. Not one bit. And she was going to find out why. What had changed her friend? It was no longer a question of not being included. Primrose guessed that she might not even want to be included in whatever Eglantine was up to, but she planned to find out what it was nonetheless. Until she knew more she would keep her thoughts to herself, but as soon as she figured it out, she would go directly to Soren. However, before she did that, she dared to ask Eglantine a question. "Eglantine, I want to know something."

"Yes. Sure. Anything, Primrose."

"What's Ginger really like?"

"What do you mean?"

"I mean it seems strange to me that she is always wanting to get you off by yourself."

"Off by myself?"

"Yeah, it's kind of like she's jealous."

"Jealous?" Eglantine blinked and stared blankly into space.

"Yeah, jealous. I don't think real friends are jealous."

"Real?"

It's useless, Primrose thought. All Eglantine did was echo back her own words. This wasn't a conversation at all. She didn't know what it was, but it certainly was not two good friends talking.

So Primrose watched carefully for several days. She noticed nothing unusual. But then a week after she had come out of the infirmary, as the days of the summer, the season of the golden rain, began to shorten and the nights grew ever longer, Primrose noticed that Eglantine often simply went off by herself during free flight after class or chaw practice.

The third time this happened, Primrose decided to follow her. It was a dark, moonless night. Thick cloud cover obscured the stars and Primrose, not the most silent of fliers, thanked a wind that ruffled off the land and across the water, muting her wingbeats. She was surprised when she saw Eglantine set off due south. It was a long stretch of water between the Island of Hoole and any land. Indeed, the first land in that direction would be The Beaks, a place that they had been warned to avoid. Mrs Plithiver was particularly outspoken about The Beaks and frequently recalled the time when she and the band went there, and the four owls had fallen into some kind of odd trance. The lakes in that region were considered beautiful but terribly dangerous. Why would Eglantine be setting off for The Beaks? What would ever draw her there? *Well,* thought Primrose, *if it takes going to The Beaks to get to the bottom of this, then I will go.* She may have been small, but she was strong – strong of wing, strong of gizzard.

So Primrose flew on. She did wonder, however, what Eglantine was carrying in her beak. It looked like papers of some sort. She hadn't had them at the beginning of free flight, but she had lighted down on some cliffs before setting out across the sea. After they had been flying a while, the cloud cover cleared off, and land appeared like a darker smudge in the distance. The distinct sharp hills of The Beaks could actually be felt before they were seen. The wind curled up from those hills in seductive thermal drafts, even in the coolness of the night. They were lovely to ride. And even on this moonless night, the fabled Mirror Lakes sparkled.

Eglantine was heading for a fir tree that grew beside one of these lakes. Primrose knew that she would have to be careful now to avoid being seen. She swooped off at an angle and found a spruce to settle in on the other side of the lake, from which she could observe Eglantine's movements. A large Barn Owl with a great shining face had come out on the limb of the fir tree.

"Mum!" Eglantine shouted.

Mum! Is she yoicks? And if this is her mum, why

hasn't she told Soren? Primrose blinked. It wasn't a scroom. It was a real feather-and-bone owl. She could tell. Eglantine handed the owl the papers she had brought.

"Darling!" she heard the owl exclaim.

Primrose strained to hear more. She had to get closer. She carefully lofted herself in short flight to a closer tree, and then a closer one.

"Any centipedes, Mum?"

"Would I forget?"

"Oh no, Mum. Of course not. Never," Eglantine said. "Where's Da?"

"Still hunting."

"And Soren too?"

"Yes, still out hunting."

Primrose blinked in utter confusion. *Soren? Out hunting in The Beaks? Soren was back at the great tree. What is happening?* And that was Primrose's second-to-last thought. Her eyes flinched. There was a blinding glare and then nothing. She felt herself being stuffed into some sort of sack.

And this was how Primrose arrived at her last thought: the sack into which she had been stuffed was the same kind in which rogue smiths often carried their tools. And once there had been a rogue smith in The Beaks. A Barred Owl. Soren, Gylfie,

Twilight and Digger had found him dying. At first, they had thought a bobcat had murdered the Barred Owl. But no, the Pure Ones, led by Kludd, had murdered him.

I shall die like the Barred Owl, I shall die.

That was Primrose's very last thought.

CHAPTER TWELVE

A Gizzard Begins to Stir

"Oh, that's an interesting book, Eglantine," Otulissa said as she came into the library. "I was just reading it the other day. It's about the correspondences between the quadrants of the gizzard and those of the brain. I do believe that the owl who had the most perfect correspondence of brain and gizzard was our dearest Strix Struma."

Eglantine flinched and then wilfed so noticeably that both Otulissa and Soren, who was also in the library, jumped towards her.

"What's wrong Eglantine?" Soren cried.

"Why did you say 'dearest'?" Eglantine asked Otulissa.

"Dearest?" Otulissa said again. "Because she was. Strix Struma was the dearest owl I have ever known."

Eglantine seemed to freeze. "Only Mum ever said that word to us, Soren. You know it."

Soren and Otulissa peered at Eglantine in complete bewilderment. "Eglantine, don't be ridiculous. You can't own a word. If Otulissa wants to use the word 'dearest' she can. Holy Glaux, what's got into you?"

"Well, why don't you call her 'darling' instead?" Eglantine said stubbornly.

"I don't like the word 'darling'. I think it's phoney and ostentatious. It sounds like some gewgaw that would be dangling all glittery in Madame Plonk's apartment. *Darling!* Yecch!" Otulissa made a disgusting sound that came from the back of her throat as if she were spitting out a bad slug.

"Give it a blow, Eglantine," Soren said. He rarely spoke rudely to his sister, but she didn't even seem to notice. And this fact intrigued Digger, who had his beak buried in a tracking book he was researching for Sylvana, the tracking ryb on whom he had an enormous crush. *Now why,* Digger thought, *did Eglantine flinch over the word 'dearest' and not when her brother was pointedly rude to her?*

Just then, Otulissa suddenly exploded. "Holy Glaux! This really frinks me off... It spr—" Otulissa seemed to be fighting with her own beak not to say the vilest swear word in owl language – the s-p-r word: sprink.

"What in the world is it, Otulissa?" Soren asked.

"Someone has ripped two pages out of this higher magnetics book."

"You're kidding!" Gylfie gasped.

"Look." Otulissa held up the book. The jagged edges of torn pages prickled up from the inside of the book like an ugly wound.

"Dewlap?" Digger said.

"She hasn't been in the library since she collapsed after Strix Struma's Last Ceremony."

"Who would do this?" Digger said. The owls looked around in utter bafflement.

But suddenly there was a great commotion outside the library sky port and Ruby flew in. "Primrose is missing!"

"What?" they all said.

"She never came back from night flight."

All their heads swung towards Eglantine. "Didn't you notice?" Soren asked.

"I came in early and went to sleep, and then this evening I got up late and thought she was already out. Gee, I hope she's all right."

Digger observed Eglantine closely. Her words sounded hollow to him.

The search-and-rescue chaw members, as well as those in tracking, were now organising the other owls to divide up into small groups to conduct a search. Because they were the most experienced, each senior member of the search-and-rescue chaw would lead owls from other chaws on the hunt. A member from the tracking chaw would accompany each group for the groundwork of finding any traces of a downed owl.

They were given only a few minutes to get ready. Eglantine rushed back to her hollow.

"What's going on?" Ginger asked her.

"Oh, it's Primrose. She seems to have got herself lost."

"Oh," Ginger said and yawned.

Eglantine blinked. For just a split second, it was as if she had stepped out of her own body, her own feathers, and was listening to herself. Why did she sound this way? *Primrose is my best friend. Why don't I feel anything? Why do I sound so weird? Am I me? Where is me?* It was almost as if a stranger inhabited her body, her gizzard. Gizzard? Did she still have one? She had not felt anything in her gizzard, not a twinge, in days, weeks!

This should panic her, she realised, but oddly it did not. *Something is wrong. Something is very strange, but why don't I care? All I care about is seeing Mum and I*

*don't even care that she forgets and calls me 'darling',
not 'Eggie' like she used to.* Even when the other owls
discovered the pages that she herself had torn out of
the higher magnetics book, Eglantine had felt nothing.
Not guilty, not happy that she had done it, although
her mum was happy when she'd brought them to her.
In truth, Eglantine didn't even know what happy was
any more, just as she didn't know what sad was. She
should be sad about Primrose. But it was just too much
trouble, too much energy to feel anything. And the
oddness of it all struck her now. Her gizzard was still
as a stone. She looked at Ginger and out of curiosity
said, "You know, Primrose is my best friend. It's funny
I don't feel sad or anything."

"Well, maybe she's not really your best friend,
Eglantine," Ginger replied. She paused and walked
up to her. "Maybe I am."

Eglantine looked at Ginger a very long time and
then squinted her eyes. "No, no. I don't think so."
And for the first time in days she felt a dim little
pulse in her gizzard.

"Suit yourself," Ginger said amiably, and turned
her back.

Eglantine had been assigned to a team of trackers
and rescuers led by Digger, who was one of the best

in the tracking chaw. Eglantine was a trainee in search-and-rescue and knew many of the basics, such as how to first scan for crows' nests in any vicinity. Crows were known to mob owls, especially owls flying alone in daylight hours. And then of course, the searchers tried to listen for any cries of distress. Barn Owls were renowned for their hearing abilities. With unevenly placed ear slits and slightly concave faces that could scoop up sounds from any direction, Barn Owls were able to detect the slightest noise – from the chirp of a lone cricket to the heartbeat of a mouse. As Eglantine flew, she felt that something was just a little off-kilter. Her sight and her hearing were not matching up as they had in the past. That was weird. Oh well. She just began to say the words to herself when she thought, *Oh well? I shouldn't be thinking 'oh well'. It can mean life or death for an owl if its hearing and its vision don't match up. I should be in a complete panic. But I'm not. What is happening to me? What has happened to me?*

"For Glaux's sake!" Martin, a little Northern Saw-whet and a good friend of Soren's, shouted at her. "Watch where you're flying, Eglantine! You nearly clipped me on that last turn."

"Sorry," she said mildly.

Digger swivelled his head around. *What is wrong*

with Eglantine? he wondered for perhaps the tenth time in the last couple of hours.

There was no sign of Primrose. They had flown out in multiple directions and found nothing. There was now talk of contacting their slipgizzles in certain regions of the Southern Kingdoms. They returned before dawn. Eglantine skipped breaklight and went directly to bed. But she did not sleep. All morning and through the afternoon she sat perched above her bed of moss and down. It was scratchier than the one that her mum had made so lovingly for her in the dream hollow. She blinked and wondered. *Is that all I feel any more, just the softness or roughness of something?* Then there was another little pulse, a twinge in her gizzard. That dream, the very real dream, it had been nice, even lovely. *I can visit the dream hollow as I please… as I please. But does it please me? And Ginger is nice, but she's not like Primrose, is she?* Primrose was never jealous. Something stirred uncomfortably in her. *Jealous.* Primrose had said that Ginger might be jealous. Friends were not jealous. But Ginger wasn't exactly a friend. *Why am I thinking this?* Eglantine wondered. And then like the bits and pieces of debris that swirled in the eddies and currents of the Sea of Hoolemere, Primrose's exact words came back to her:

"Yeah, jealous. I don't think real friends are jealous."

Real! Something wasn't real. As if playing with a puzzle, Eglantine began assembling the scattered pieces. Real... Primrose is real. A real friend. Ginger is not quite real... Dreams are not real... Then she thought about her mum. And then about Ginger some more. And dreams. Could dreams be prisons? What if she didn't want to be in this dream? Would her mum just melt away? Would she even care? After all, Eglantine didn't really care about anything any more. So what would it matter? Her thoughts went around and around, and she always came back to the same thought: nothing really mattered. Suddenly she realised that she was caught in a dream that she could not escape. And now her gizzard gave a huge lurch. How could she escape? How could she make herself care? How could she find what was real again?

To escape the dream, I must look into my dream mum's eyes. I must look behind her eyes. I must see what is real and what is not. I must go back one last time. A terrible dread began to swim through Eglantine's gizzard.

And she was glad.

CHAPTER THIRTEEN

The Lucky Charm

Primrose blinked. It was daylight now. So the night was done. She wondered if the owls at the great tree had missed her yet. And what about Eglantine? Was she still here or had she gone back? She was not sure how long she had been in the hollow, but at least they had let her out of the bag. A Sooty Owl, a species related to Barn Owls but more grey than buff-coloured, stuck his head in. "I have orders for you to go to sleep. Settle down in that nest, now. You'll never sleep on any finer moss. And she plucked down from her own breast for you and arranged it herself."

How kind! thought Primrose. "What if I don't want to sleep?"

The Sooty Owl blinked and then made a series of clicking sounds that Primrose supposed was to intimidate her. "It's not a question of what you want. It's an order."

"In the Great Ga'Hoole Tree we get to sleep when we want to."

"Well guess what, Sweet Tuft. You ain't in Ga'Hoole any more."

"I take it I am among the Pure Ones," Primrose replied.

"You take what you want. Now get to sleep," the Sooty snarled.

Primrose flew up to an interior perch and lighted down. "Not there. Down here in the nice fluffy bed."

"I sleep better on a perch."

"Down in the nest! And that's an order."

Primrose never heard of anything so ridiculous. Why was it so important where she slept in this hollow? She was a prisoner no matter what. So she settled into the nest, which indeed did have the softest, fluffiest moss she had ever experienced. But despite the luxurious trimming of this nest, she could not get comfortable. She then sensed a strange buzzing in her head and her gizzard seemed to grow still. She stepped away from the nest and the buzzing stopped. Pygmy Owls, weighing less than two ounces and measuring just a sliver more than fifteen centimetres long, are extremely sensitive to environmental changes that might not affect larger owls. And as soon as she stepped away she felt her gizzard change. She lifted one talon and touched the approximate place where her gizzard was lodged. She tried to picture in her mind Otulissa's diagram with the quadrants. She remembered reading the book on humours and discussing it with Ezylryb as he explained about the four basic humours. Ezylryb's words came back to her.

"You know how in all of our brains there are tiny bits of magnetic particles much smaller than flecks. They are sometimes called iron oxides. They aid us with navigation because they help us feel the earth's magnetic field. Imagine, however, if something disturbed those bits in our brain..."

Something is disturbing my brain, Primrose thought. *And something is happening to my gizzard as well.* She vividly remembered Ezylryb's mangled talon pointing to the diagram. In an older owl, exposure to flecks could disturb the humours and cause navigational problems, but in a younger owl like herself – yes, and like Eglantine – it could shatter all internal systems. Ezylryb's words were so clear now it was as if the old Whiskered Screech's voice was inside her own head.

The gizzard itself becomes almost like stone, incapable of sorting out feelings and emotions. It can even cause delusions. That is what fleckasia is all about.

Primrose now knew: she was being shattered, and Eglantine already had been!

"Hey!" the Sooty Owl called in. "Didn't I tell you to bed down? Do I have to come in there and sit on you?"

At your own risk, thought Primrose. She had to stall for time. "Sure, sure, just have to yarp a pellet," she answered.

"Well yarp and get to sleep." Then she heard the Sooty give a big yawn.

She went to a corner of the hollow to yarp. She felt better as soon as the pellet came up, but she wasn't sure if it was because of relieving herself of the pellet or just stepping away from the nest. Obviously, flecks had been embedded in the nest materials. Then she remembered several times when she had awakened in her hollow at the Great Ga'Hoole Tree and Eglantine had been restless with her supposedly 'lovely' dreams. An image came back to her. It was Ginger bent over Eglantine, patting her as if to soothe her, but maybe she was not soothing her. Maybe she was poking in flecks. Glaux knew where she got them.

"Finished with that yarp yet? Now back to bed or I'm calling Her Pureness."

Oh Glaux, Primrose thought. *I am right in the middle of something really bad*. She had to think fast. She couldn't scatter the nest because the flecks would drift all over the place. She touched the amber bead that she wore around her neck. *Good-luck charm*, she thought. *Well, show your stuff*. She rubbed it absently with one of her tiny talons, then let the chain it hung from drop back down on her breast feathers. She felt an odd ruffle and looked down. She blinked. All the soft feathers in which the amber bead lay were sticking straight out. She blinked again. She had never seen her feathers or any owl's feathers do that.

"Get to bed."

"All right, all right."

The light in the hollow was quite dim and outside it was very bright. If this Sooty was keeping watch on her, he would have to constantly adjust his eyes because of the contrast of light. The first idea that came to Primrose was to arrange herself in the nest so that the back of her head was facing the Sooty. A Pygmy Owl had two dark, feathery spots on the back of its head that were called eyespots. For owls not accustomed to flying behind a Pygmy, these eyespots could be disorientating and cause confusion. With the back of her head facing him, she could examine the amber bead more carefully, which was exactly what she planned to do. She crouched down in the pile of moss and downy fluff. Once more, the buzzing began to niggle into her head. But Primrose was determined. She rubbed the amber again. The feathers stood up and she felt a slight prickling sensation. Not only that, but a small bit of moss seemed to almost jump to the amber drop. That was interesting. She tried it again. *Glaux!* There was all sorts of stuff clinging to the amber bead. *This can't be a magnet. It's not iron or even magnetic rock.* She knew that from her metal class with Bubo. Amber was fossilised sap from an evergreen tree. And what could amber do? *Holy Glaux in glaumora, it's charged. I rubbed it, and it's become charged!*

Primrose realised if the amber wasn't a magnet, how else would things be drawn to it? It must have been her rubbing it that did it. Yes, Bubo had often called amber 'fool's iron', and she guessed if you rubbed it, it became a sort of magnet. *So if I rub this hard enough and often enough and then poke it down into the moss, what will happen?* Primrose removed the bead of amber from her neck and, holding on to the chain, let it drop into the piles of moss and down.

A moment later Primrose had her answer. She pulled up the chain and the bead of amber was bristling with hundreds of tiny flecks. Now, how could she get rid of the foul stuff? She knew that fire destroyed the magnetic properties of flecks and left them harmless, but she could hardly start a fire in here. She looked around. There was a niche in the tree where some bore worms must have been feeding. She supposed she could scrape the flecks off into that. She just had to get them away from her head. After all, she suddenly realised, she had slept in the same hollow with Eglantine and had suffered no ill effects.

So Primrose began excavating the flecks, but she thought of it more as fishing than excavating. Each time she pulled up the chain, very quietly so as not to alert the guard, it was bristling with flecks. It took twelve times for the amber bead to finally come up clean. "You really are my lucky charm," she whispered.

And now, she thought, *all I have to do is pretend that I am shattered.* She remembered Soren and Gylfie explaining to her how they had pretended to be moon blinked when they were imprisoned in St Aggie's. Well, she would pretend to be shattered. After all, she had a very fine example to follow – Eglantine. And with the thought of her friend, Primrose's gizzard twisted in the most agonising way.

CHAPTER FOURTEEN

As a Gizzard Twitches

It had been three days since Primrose had disappeared. Everyone had different theories. Otulissa was sure that it was an indication that the Pure Ones were active again.

"Why the Pure Ones?" Soren asked. "Why not St Aggie's?" They were in their hollow having a light snack of dried caterpillars as it would be another hour until tweener.

"I can't imagine them coming this far north," Gylfie said.

"What would they want with Primrose?" Twilight asked.

"I'm not sure, but Primrose is smart. I've been in

the library with her a lot lately. She catches on quick. She was really interested in quadrant theory," Otulissa replied.

"Quadrant theory?" Twilight asked.

"You know, the stuff Ezylryb was telling us about the humours," Otulissa said.

"The Pure Ones don't want to know about quadrant theory," Soren said emphatically. "They want to know about flecks. They want to know about how, with higher magnetics, you can make other things fleck-full, and how, with a dowsing rod, you can find flecks. They want to control all the flecks in the world."

"But don't you see, Soren, it's all connected," Otulissa said. "Remember when we were at St Aggie's and they were tucking the flecks into the nests in the eggorium? The Pure Ones were doing that. It's not just flecks they want to control, it's minds – mind control."

Digger suddenly flew in through the sky port. He dropped Otulissa's dowsing rod on the floor of the hollow.

"What are you doing with my dowsing rod?"

"I'm sorry I didn't ask, Otulissa, but I had a hunch."

"Well, I hope it was a good hunch," she said huffily.

"It was a good hunch, but I am afraid I have very bad news."

"What?" Soren had a terrible feeling deep within him. His gizzard began to tremble.

"Soren, I have been feeling for a while that something is wrong with Eglantine – more than just summer flux. You know, because Eglantine had once before been imprisoned by the Pure Ones, and her mind had been disturbed then... Well—" Digger hesitated. "I think she is perhaps even more vulnerable."

Soren was so frightened he couldn't even blink.

"You see, I took the dowsing rod into her hollow. Soren, it went crazy when I passed it over her nest. The place where she sleeps – it's loaded with flecks."

Otulissa wilfed suddenly. "The Pure Ones have infiltrated us!" she cried. "And they know more about flecks than we have ever imagined. They know how to shatter. Eglantine has been shattered," she said with horror.

"Eglantine's gone," Digger added.

"Gone?" Soren asked. "Gone where?"

"I don't know. But Ginger is gone too."

The alert was given for the search-and-rescue chaw to prepare. There would be two empty spots in their flying formation because now both Primrose and Eglantine were gone. It was Barran herself, the Snowy Owl and monarch of the tree, who led this chaw. Soren was determined to appeal to her and ask if he could fly with the chaw. Twilight was another member of this chaw.

"I don't know if it will work, Soren," Twilight said slowly.

"Look, they need another owl. You're short by two," Soren replied.

"But maybe you'll get too emotional. It's your sister, after all."

"Too emotional for what, Twilight?" Soren spat out the words. "Too emotional to fly? To see? To hear?"

Twilight knew then that Soren could not bear to wait in the tree for news of his sister.

Ten minutes later, Soren had stated his case to Barran. The dignified Snowy peered at him and blinked. Soren's gizzard clenched. Would she say yes or no?

"So you would like to fly as a replacement for either Eglantine or Primrose?"

"Well, I know I can't exactly replace Primrose. I mean she's a Pygmy owl, after all."

"Precisely." Soren's heart and gizzard began to sink somewhere towards his talons. "I mean, how good are you at low-level flight, threading your way through tall grass? You know those Pygmies are noisy when they fly, but you cannot beat them for low-level precision surveillance."

"Yes, yes, I suppose that's true, but..." Soren's voice trailed off.

Barran blinked, then her eyes softened and the yellow light streaming from them was like the delicate pale light of the sun in the earliest morning, in that small fraction of a second when it first slips above the horizon. "I'll tell you what, my dear. How about we get Gylfie to fly Primrose's position?"

"But... but... what about me?"

"Hush, Soren, hear me out. Elf Owls are as good as Pygmies at this low-level stuff, and I propose that you fly left ear. Eglantine had been covering that spot."

"You mean, I can go?" *Try not to be too emotional. Try not to cry. Oh Glaux! Don't cry in front of her!* But if he could get Eglantine back, even shattered, he swore to himself he would put her back together, piece by piece.

Piece by piece? Soren wondered why these words reminded him of something. Something very dim and shadowy. *Piece by piece.* The words nagged at the edges of his mind, prickling his gizzard. *Well, no time for wondering now. Time for action.*

*   *   *

Fifteen minutes later the search-and-rescue chaw lifted off with Soren flying in the spot normally occupied by Eglantine. They had no idea where they might find either one of the missing owls, but Barran thought that since both Eglantine and Primrose had been ill this summer, chances were they would not fly into an opposing wind. The wind had been blowing north by northeast, a perfect wind for Cape Glaux, the site of the great massing of the Pure Ones months before. What a scene that had been, Soren thought.

The Chaw of Chaws had been sent on a covert mission to penetrate St Aggie's. The Chaw of Chaws was the special force comprised of the band along with Otulissa, Ruby and Martin. On their return from the mission, they had heard the rumour that owls were massing on Cape Glaux and, indeed, they had been! There had been close to a thousand Pure Ones that Kludd had recruited for his invasion and siege of the Island of Hoole and the Great Ga'Hoole Tree. The Pure Ones had long since evacuated the cape as a base. There were rumours of them in a region known as Beyond the Beyond, but others had placed them in the Desert of Kuneer. They were all rumours, however, and now Soren reminded himself that they were not looking for great massings of Pure Ones, but for one very tiny Pygmy Owl and his own sister, who was shattered by the deadly power of the flecks. "Full-blown fleckasia," Otulissa had called it.

The coastline of the cape began to appear as a blurred line jutting out into the sea. They would make their landfall on a more or less protected beach within a bay called The Bight. There were some good trees that would afford perches for a rest before they began scouring the landscape in a tiered formation of low-level, mid-level and high fliers.

It has to work, Soren thought. *It just has to work.* He had lost Eglantine once. But he would not lose her twice! Twice would be too cruel to endure.

The dread that Eglantine had first felt when she realised that she was caught in a dream from which she could not wake up had continued to build. As she flew into the headwinds that tossed up slop from the Sea of Hoolemere, there was one thought that she tried to keep in her mind. She repeated it again and again. *I must look into my dream mum's eyes, I must look behind her eyes. I must see what is real and what is not. I must go back one last time.*

"Eglantine!" Ginger shouted out. "I don't understand why we couldn't have waited a few hours for this weather to pass. Why now? This stuff is hard to fly through. Your mum will still be there."

She'd better be, Eglantine thought. But was it really her mother? She began thinking of the very small differences, starting with the words her dream mum used, and her face. Had her mother's face been quite that white? And why was her da never there?

The two owls flew on. The weather grew worse. Ginger was having a hard time. But finally the coastline of The Beaks appeared. Soon they were flying over the Mirror Lakes.

I should have known... I should have known, Eglantine thought. Hadn't Mrs Plithiver told her about the Mirror Lakes of The Beaks and the strange spell they had cast on Soren, Gylfie, Twilight and Digger? The gleaming surface of the water had dazzled them and they had become fascinated by their own reflections – hypnotised, Mrs P had said. It was a dangerous place. *And now*, thought Eglantine, *it is a dangerous place with dangerous owls*. Once more, she felt a jolt run through her gizzard. *Dangerous? My mum dangerous? How strange.*

She was now approaching the fir tree. She knew she had to appear normal – but what was normal? How long had it been since she had been normal? A fog was beginning to lift in Eglantine's brain, but it took enormous energy not to sink back into it.

"Darling!" her mum called out. "Oh, I'm so pleased. And in this bad weather. Oh, how lovely that you came."

My real mum would scold me for flying in this bad weather.

"Come in. I have your favourite snack waiting for you – centipedes. But darling Eglantine. No papers for me? You know how much I enjoy the papers you bring me."

"Uh... it was raining, you know. I thought they might get wet."

"Oh yes, of course, silly me. Your da is always saying I'm such a silly old thing."

"He does?" Eglantine said blankly. "Are you sure?" Suddenly, the big white-faced owl blinked at her as if watching her more closely. *Uh-oh! Be careful.* Eglantine's gizzard quivered with fear. But the quivers felt almost good, because each time her gizzard stirred, she began to feel more like her old self.

"I have a wonderful surprise for you."

"A surprise? Da? Soren?" Eglantine blinked and looked closely. *Is she my mum? Really? How can I tell for sure?*

Primrose could hear their conversation. She was being held in a hollow just off the one in which

Eglantine and the Barn Owl were talking. She blinked her eyes. What in Glaux's name was Eglantine talking about? How could Soren or her da be here, and why was Eglantine calling this female owl 'Mum'? Primrose had seen and heard all this before when she had first arrived, just before she had been stuffed into the sack. She could hardly believe her ears then, and now she was hearing it all again!

So far, Primrose had not only resisted shattering but given a fairly decent impression of a shattered owl. She had even managed to affect that glassy, unblinking look that she had noticed in Eglantine. At first, she thought it was a symptom left over from the summer flux, but now she knew better. It was the look of a shattered owl. She was sure. But still the fact remained that she was a prisoner, and so was Eglantine for that matter. Because even though Eglantine's body was free to fly back and forth between this hollow and the Great Ga'Hoole Tree, her mind was completely enslaved to these owls. And they were the Pure Ones. They were not here in full force, but there were enough of them to make escape almost impossible. Metal Beak and apparently hundreds of others were off on some mission.

Otulissa was right; they should have launched an attack as soon as they could after the siege of last winter. They had to fight offensively. But how in Glaux's name could a two-ounce seven-inch Pygmy Owl fight these monsters by herself?

Primrose leaned closer to the opening, trying to catch more of the strange conversation going on in the hollow below.

The wind howled. The fir tree at the edge of the Mirror Lake rattled ferociously.

"Odd for The Beaks," the large Barn Owl said. "But now for the surprise," she said to Eglantine. But then she looked up and emitted a sharp *shree*. Something tumbled down out of a hole above that led to another hollow. There was a blur of feathers. Eglantine blinked. There, standing before her right next to Ginger, was Primrose. The two owls stared at each other, displaying neither shock nor dismay.

"Here is your little friend now," the Barn Owl said. She looked from Eglantine to Primrose and back again. "Are you surprised? I always like to encourage friendship, you know."

Eglantine felt a dreadful quiver in her gizzard.

"Hi," said Primrose softly. Eglantine didn't quite know how to respond. She had so many questions. Why were Primrose's eyes so glassy? It was Primrose, wasn't it? Or was it a dream Primrose like her dream mum? Eglantine's gizzard began to twitch as it had not in weeks. Her mother set out some centipedes, and then turned to Primrose and to Ginger.

"Eglantine and I always sing the centipede song together, don't we darling?"

Eglantine swung her head towards the large Barn Owl. Her black gaze bore into this dream mother. And one thought filled her brain: *would I rather live in a world without my mum and da or in a world with a dream mum?* She knew the answer. In that infinitesimal sliver of a second, the world became clear to Eglantine.

"It's Eggie! Mum called me Eggie. NOT DARLING!" she roared. Eglantine now knew that this was not her mum, nor just any dream mum. This was Nyra, the deadly mate of Kludd. And now Nyra was moving towards her with a savage look in her eyes. Her beak dropped open, ready to stab. Then an immense crack split the night. Primrose felt every feather on her body stand up. Eglantine stared as Nyra's feathers stuck stiffly straight out from her body and quivered. Next there was a terrible sizzling sound, and the fir tree burst into flames.

CHAPTER FIFTEEN

Piece by Piece

Ezylryb and his weather-and-colliering chaw perched in the highest branches of the Great Ga'Hoole Tree. The weather was foul, but nonetheless they tried to look out across the Sea of Hoolemere. Legions of electrical storms like attendants for a monarch had been accompanying this late-season hurricane that had swirled out of the warm waters of the southernmost region of the sea. Ezylryb had been expecting something like this. All summer his weather probes, a series of devices and experiments, had shown unusually warm water. Hurricanes fed on warm water.

Next to Ezylryb perched Soren, frantic with worry over his sister and Primrose. *They could be anywhere out there in this beastly weather,* he thought. And the two young owls were completely inexperienced in flying the unpredictable – and often lethal – winds of a hurricane. Soren himself had flown in only one, and it had really been just the raggedy fringes of a hurricane at that. But it had been bad enough.

The search-and-rescue mission for Primrose and Eglantine had been called off due to the weather. But... Soren almost dared not give words to the thought. He turned his head slightly towards Ezylryb. Was the old Whiskered Screech thinking of launching a weather-and-colliering chaw mission? With all the electrical storms, there were bound to be forest fires. Bubo's forge was low on the kind of coals he liked the best, the hottest ones, which burned with a fierce energy and were full of what blacksmiths called bonk. If it hadn't been for the great abundance of bonkful coals last winter, they never would have survived the siege of the Pure Ones. But of course Soren was hoping to find not just bonk coals but also his sister and the dear little Pygmy Owl, Primrose, whom he had met on his very first night in the Great Ga'Hoole Tree when she had been brought in dazed from a fire in her home forest of Silverveil. Just as Soren was thinking about all this, Bubo lighted down on the limb.

"What'cha think, Cap?" Bubo asked.

"Can't see much from here. Not the course of its river at least."

Soren knew that what Ezylryb meant by 'its river' was the constantly moving and changing air that was embedded deep in a hurricane and, as it flowed, directed its course. "From here, it's hard to see much. I think I see a smudge of rosy light stretching from The Barrens to maybe even The Beaks."

"Huh, that be curious," Bubo said. "The Beaks. Usually sweet as spring there. Nary a storm nor even the slightest thundershower."

The Beaks! Even though it had been long ago that Soren and his band had been caught in its deadly charm, The Beaks still struck fear in him. Surely Ezylryb was not thinking of going to The Beaks. It was known to be a dangerous place for owls with its mesmerising beauty, softest moss, plentiful game and the shimmering Mirror Lakes.

"Heh!" snorted Ezylryb. "Imagine that! The Beaks on fire. Very curious. Might want to see that myself."

Soren exchanged glances with Otulissa.

"The Beaks," Otulissa whispered. "The Beaks is the last place we need to go."

Soren knew exactly what Otulissa was thinking. She wanted to go to the Northern Kingdoms, specifically to the Kielian League to gather forces to help fight the Pure Ones, but so far no one had paid much attention to her idea. She spent unbelievable amounts of time in the library, researching the Northern Kingdoms and all their various clans.

Later, a decision was made, and as twilight stole over the sea and the Island of Hoole was wrapped in the first purpling of the night, a chaw rose into the sky. It was not just any chaw, however. At its very centre was the Chaw of Chaws. Perhaps this had been Ezylryb and Barran's strategy from the beginning, when the Snowy monarch of the tree suggested that Gylfie fly with search-and-rescue and then Ezylryb suggested that the weather-and-colliering chaw reconnoitre the possibility of forest fires in The Beaks. Maybe it had all been a grand scheme to assemble the band in addition to Ruby, Martin and Otulissa for an action that was more extensive than finding two lost owls. Soren didn't know, but he felt more confident than he had in the last three days as they circled and climbed higher over the Sea of Hoolemere and set a course for The Beaks.

"South by southeast," Gylfie shouted out. Now, in addition to her usual navigation responsibilities, she had to fly low-level for search-and-rescue.

The hurricane was far to the southwest of them but was causing unstable weather throughout most of the

Southern Kingdoms. Massive thunderheads piled up like mountains around them, and as they approached the coast they threaded their way through a string of electrical storms that were setting forests on fire. It was unimaginable to Soren that either Eglantine or Primrose could fly through this kind of brutal weather. Lightning cracked the sky, flaying the blackness of the night. "Showing its bones," as owls said. Each time a bolt sent its jagged white fire across the night, Soren flinched. That whiteness bothered him. Why? He'd flown through electrical storms before. It was all part of being a member of the weather chaw. There was another crack. The blackness was fractured once more by the bony streaks of lightning, and just above the horizon, it looked as if a deranged skeleton were dancing an eerie jig across the night sky.

Ezylryb dropped back from the point position and slipped in next to Soren.

"The path of this hurricane and its speed make me think that the most logical place Eglantine and Primrose would be blown is towards The Beaks. Hurricanes, as you know, go anti-clockwise, so if it gives you any peace of mind they would at least be on the less turbulent side of it."

But it didn't give Soren much peace of mind because ahead the coast of The Beaks raged with fires. And Eglantine and Primrose knew very little about navigating through forest fires. *Some choice*, he thought, *being battered to death by a hurricane or being fried by a forest fire!*

Twilight, who was flying point, now called out, "Mirror Lakes ahead!"

And for the band the words were like an electrical current crackling through their gizzards.

Soren blinked. *I shall not be transfixed. I shall not be charmed. I shall not yield!* Below him, the usually still and gleaming silver surfaces of the lakes danced frantically with the reflections of flames.

"Great Glaux!" Gylfie gasped. "It looks like hagsmire."

Indeed, Soren thought he was looking into the very heart of owl hell. The flames dancing across the surface might have been the devils of that hell, the hagsfiends that flew with not two wings but dozens, all tipped with fire. Was this yet a new way that the lakes could work their deadly charms? It could be like fire blinking, the most dreaded trick that fire could pull on a collier. This happened when the fire, raging with all its deadly beauty, transfixed an owl so that it could not fly. The owl went yeep, lost all instincts to fly, and suddenly plummeted to the ground or, in this case, into the water to drown.

Then suddenly there was a loud clap of thunder and a bolt of lightning hissed down towards the lake, momentarily bleaching the dance of flames a luminous, violent white. And in that split second, Soren's forgotten dream of early summer burst upon him – piece by piece by piece: the fog; the sea afloat with fragments of paper; suddenly finding himself not over the sea but The Beaks; the lakes shattering into hundreds of dazzling shards; their blinding whiteness reminding him of something; the feeling of dread. No time to wonder. Then his vow "I'll take these lakes – piece by piece. Yes, Mrs Plithiver, piece by piece by piece."

But now he knew what the whiteness was. "Nyra!" He screeched, and he thought of Eglantine and Primrose. Piece by piece by piece that evil owl had captured them, their minds, their instincts, and now their bodies!

CHAPTER SIXTEEN

The Sacred Orb

"The Sacred Orb!" screeched Nyra. "Do you have it?
Do you have it?"

"Worry not, Madame," a lieutenant called Stryker
replied. "It is tucked safely in the flight pouch."

"I'll peck out the eyes of the one who drops it! And
then their gizzard!" Nyra said in a deadly voice.

"Fear not, Madame Pureness. Fear not," another
Pure Guard shouted over the roar of the flames.

"Can we find a safe tree?" asked Ginger.

Eglantine and Primrose were being flanked by
several guards. There was no possibility of escape.
And most shockingly, there was Ginger with a
disgusting smirk on her face. Eglantine should have

known. Primrose was right about Ginger all along.

When the tree burst into flames, they had all been blown out in the same direction, and then before they knew it the guards had closed in on them. Now what was this talk of a sacred orb? Strange words, and Eglantine was not at all sure what they meant. But she couldn't think about that now. She had to think about how to get herself and Primrose out of this fix. *Primrose looks odd. What have they done to her?*

"Safe tree!" a guard called out. "Safe tree ahead!"

Before them was an enormous oak that had been singed by the fire but had never actually ignited. It now loomed in the scorched and red-stained night. A hollow opening, not large but adequate, revealed itself midway up the tree. The Pure Guards shoved Eglantine and Primrose roughly through the opening.

"First the Sacred Orb and then I'll tend to you!" Nyra swivelled her head and glared at Eglantine.

"Here, Madame Pureness." A large Barn Owl stepped forward. Eglantine was stunned as her eyes fell on a Barn Owl egg, glistening white and perfectly round. The other guards folded their legs and dipped their heads in an odd and awkward movement.

"Bow down!" Nyra *shree*d at Eglantine and Primrose. "Bow down, for this is your future ruler. Your blessing. Your curse. Your new Glaux Most Pure."

Eglantine and Primrose blinked and bowed as best they could.

"I'll need some more moss for the Sacred Orb's nest. I have used practically all my down. Gort, you and Tonk go out and fetch some moss – rabbit ear if you can find it." Rabbit ear moss was the softest of all the mosses, and scarce. "Nothing but the best for Little Purity," she said softly, but her eyes had a hard, fierce gleam like no mother's eyes Eglantine or Primrose had ever seen.

Then Nyra stepped towards Eglantine in the cramped space. Her white face was streaked with soot. Her black eyes bore into Eglantine. "She knows." Although Nyra faced Eglantine, it was as if she were directing her words to the Pure Guards. There was a deadly calm in her voice. "She knows that I am not her mother. That I am Her Pureness. Right, my darling?" And the word 'darling' curled like the meanest snarl in the close space of the hollow. Eglantine wilfed. She became almost half her size and her gizzard quaked as it never had before.

Primrose stole a glance at her with an odd mixture of fear and relief. Relief to see that her old friend was back, seemingly restored to her senses. *But*, thought Primrose, *Nyra doesn't know what I know. She doesn't know that I am not shattered.* And then Primrose wondered if Eglantine realised it. She had to keep up the act, but was there any way she could let Eglantine know that it was just an act, that she was all right? If she could, there was a chance that somehow they could escape, but they would have to work together.

"I should have suspected," said Ginger suddenly. "When she wanted to fly in this weather, I should have known something was up."

"That it was more than just mother love?" Nyra stepped closer to Eglantine. "Mother looove," she dragged out the word. "More like Mummy's dummy!" she sneered and cackled. The Pure Guards joined in with soft churrings. Without taking her eyes off Elgantine, Nyra again directed a question to the Pure Guards. "But this one—" She cocked her head towards Primrose. "Is she properly shattered?"

"Yes, Your Pureness." The Sooty Owl who had guarded Primrose stepped forward. "Good and proper, Madame Pureness."

"Oh no!" Eglantine moaned.

"Oh yes," Nyra paused. "*Darling!*"

Fear not, Eglantine. Fear not! Primrose thought. *Oh, if only there was a way I could send her a message, some code, anything! If only I could think of something.*

But it wasn't Primrose who thought of something. It was Eglantine. Her eyes fastened on the gleaming egg. Where, she wondered, had Nyra hidden it the many times she had come to visit? There was no telling when this egg had been laid, or how close it was to hatching. *If I could someway, somehow get that egg, Nyra would go yeep. More than yeep! Great Glaux, all the Pure Ones would be in our power if we had the egg!*

Eglantine, after all, had been trained for search-and-rescue and the members of this chaw were known for their talon dexterity. They were often required to pluck owl chicks from the forest floor. Many times these chicks were injured and they had to be handled with extreme care.

Think, Eglantine! Think! The words silently thundered in her brain. Nyra turned to her once more and spoke in that voice that despite its slow calm tone was somehow like a blade cutting the air. "I am down, as it were, to my last fluff of down. My breast is sore and nearly bare from providing the lining for the Sacred Orb's nest. I feel that you should contribute to your little nephew's or perhaps your niece's comfort." She nodded towards Eglantine's breast feathers. It was a shocking suggestion. Nyra laughed as she saw the dismay on Eglantine's face.

Wait, Eglantine suddenly thought. *This is it! My chance!*

"Start plucking!" Nyra ordered.

Eglantine stepped up to where the egg rested.

"Bow before you approach."

"Oh, sorry," Eglantine said in her most submissive voice, and once more began to perform the awkward little bowing manoeuvre. Her shoulders shook and she seemed to cringe, which Nyra observed with pleasure. *I must bow deeper this time. This is it. This is it! I have to move fast.*

Primrose looked on, trying to maintain the glassy stare of a shattered owl, but something was prickling her gizzard. *She's going to do something. I just know it. I have to be ready!*

Then it was as if Eglantine's and Primrose's minds merged, their gizzards were in harmony, and together they grew bold. With her back to the rest of the owls as she bowed, neither Nyra nor any other owl could see what Eglantine was doing. Under the deception of a most obsequious bow, Eglantine's talons extended, her two back toes reversing direction as all owl toes can, giving her a powerful grip. Eglantine did not simply stand up from her bowed position, she launched herself like a feathered missile straight out of the hollow's opening. Primrose was on her tail.

"They've escaped!" Nyra *shree*d in a stunned voice.

"Worse than that, Madame Pureness, the Sacred Orb is gone!"

"Nooooooooooooooo!"

And Nyra, although she was not flying, went yeep and fell over in a dead faint.

Into the darkness the two young owls flew. "I'm right beside you, Eglantine," Primrose said.

"You're not shattered?"

"No," she replied.

"You're a stronger owl than me."

"No time to talk. They'll be after us in a minute."

Primrose saw Eglantine cock her head in the inimitable manner of Barn Owls as she tried to orient to a sound. *They must be coming already!* Primrose thought.

"They're coming in from the west, about two points off my tail, above us but still behind by less than half a league."

The smoke seemed to be growing thicker. Primrose suddenly had an idea. "How good are you at low-level flight, Eglantine?"

"Not as good as a Pygmy or an Elf, that's for sure."

"Yeah, but you can do it. Remember that lark in the dark, that meadow we went through last spring? You were great for a Barn Owl."

"For a Barn Owl maybe, but..."

"But nothing! We're being chased by Barn Owls, and you're better than they are."

Eglantine supposed this might be true. The Pure Ones, being so pure and all, had probably never just gone off larking about with lowly Pygmy owls.

"And I have another idea," Primrose said excitedly.

"What's that?"

"The smoke is getting really thick. Smoke rises. We go down low, close to the ground. The air will be clearer but they won't be able to see us as well."

Smart! Eglantine marvelled at her best friend's quick thinking.

"Hang on to that egg and let's go!" Primrose descended in a breathtaking inverted spike. Eglantine followed.

Above them, they heard the screech of not just the few Barn Owls who had been in the hollow but what sounded like an entire squadron. It was one of the Pure Ones' elite forces – the Nyra Annihilators.

How long can we last with them on our tails? Eglantine dared not guess. *Oh, Glaux! Let the smoke stay!*

CHAPTER SEVENTEEN

The Hostage Egg

It was Otulissa who had first told Soren that he must have starsight. He and Martin had been in a fierce and brutal encounter with the moonfaced owl. They had survived, but barely. As soon as the moonfaced owl and the other attackers had been driven off, he realised that he had dreamed of this very same moonfaced owl called Nyra before he had met her in battle. He had dreamed of the encounter in an odd, fragmented way that had made no sense to him at the time. He told Otulissa about the dream later. She was quiet for a moment and then looked at him curiously. "You have what they call the starsight," she said. "You dream about things and sometimes they happen. The stars for you are like little holes in the cloth of a dream." Otulissa had told him it was a gift. But it was a very strange gift, and one that stirred his gizzard with the deepest of fears.

So when this dream from early summer came back to him, piece by piece by piece, it all began to make dreadful sense. And because the members of the Chaw of Chaws and the other owls of Ga'Hoole knew of Soren's strange gift, they listened to him. It was Soren who now flew in the point position, and it was Soren who now gave the command to Gylfie and another small Elf Owl along with Digger and assorted trackers to begin to fly low.

"We need all the low fliers we can get," he said. "If you can fly beneath this smoke you'll see more." In Soren's dream, there had been a brief clear place that he had flown into where the air was limpid – free of smoke and almost translucent. They had to get to that place now.

Huddled in a hole beneath a large rotted-out tree stump, Eglantine and Primrose peered out and up into the thick layers of smoke.

"You were right, Primrose. It's pretty clear down here. I hope they don't get the same idea. That squadron is scary."

"Well so are we," Primrose said defiantly. "Let's just hope that the smoke doesn't clear off for a while." She paused. "We've got to think."

The situation was complicated. If it cleared off they could be found. But if they could steal away under the cover of the smoke and somehow get out over the Sea of Hoolemere with the egg, well, then they would be almost home free. And what power they would have. Eglantine looked down at the egg. *I'm an aunt!* The idea seemed very weird. Who knew how this owl chick would hatch out? A monster like its parents? And if it weren't, what chance would it have? It was all very sad. If they could get the egg back to the Great Ga'Hoole Tree, the poor thing might have a chance at a decent life. Eglantine began to think about eggs and chicks and hatching and what made owls the way they were. Why had she and Soren been born one way and Kludd another? Mrs Plithiver had said that from the time he had first hatched, Kludd was trouble. He had been insanely jealous. *How is one born jealous?* Distracted by these thoughts, Eglantine had not noticed that the smoke above them was thinning.

"Great Glaux, it's clearing!" Primrose exclaimed.

"Oh no!" Eglantine looked up nervously. She could see the sky, which meant the Pure Ones could see them.

"Maybe we'll be safe here. This hole is pretty well hidden. Can we go deeper into it?" Primrose asked, trying to sound calm.

"I'll check," Eglantine said. "Watch the egg. But it might not be a good idea to go deeper. They could trap us."

"You're right," Primrose replied in a taut voice.

"Maybe there's a back way out. I'll see if the hole tunnels through to the other side," Eglantine said as she started cautiously down the hole. *Too bad I'm not a Burrowing Owl*, she thought.

Eglantine was back in a short time. "It does!"

"But then I suppose that means they could surround us and come in through both sides."

"Oh Glaux! I never thought of that. I don't want to be trapped."

"I don't either, but we do have the egg," Primrose said.

"What do you mean by that?"

"Well, the egg's worth a lot to them. We could probably trade them the egg and get out."

Eglantine blinked, then her eyes seemed to narrow and grow harder and even blacker. "I wouldn't trust them in any kind of trade. And besides, the egg is worth even more to us and all the owl kingdoms. With it, we can control the Pure Ones. We can't give it up."

"You mean it's a hostage?"

"Exactly!"

Now Primrose blinked at Eglantine. In that moment, she knew that Eglantine had changed. It was as if she had suddenly grown much, much older. She would sacrifice her life for that egg. She would die to save that egg from the Pure Ones. Until that moment, Eglantine had only thought about death as depriving her of something she loved – her mother, her father, the place she had once called home. But now Primrose knew that Eglantine realised that you could die for something. You could die for something you loved. You could die fighting against something you hated. You could die for freedom, the freedom of the owl kingdoms.

"I see them, Primrose. I see them," Eglantine whispered.

The two owls huddled closer and pressed themselves deeper under the stump.

The smoke was clearing. Nyra had her vision back and now she would use her powerful abilities to hear. She must find her egg. Thus the moonfaced owl began to swivel her head in smooth and precise movements, scanning for not just any sound, but a very special one that only owl mothers are attuned to.

She filtered out the sound of a mouse's heartbeat as it skittered across the forest floor, and that of a snake slithering over a log. There was the laboured breathing of a mother rabbit as she gave birth to a new litter. *Bunnies, yum!* Nyra thought, but then admonished herself to listen for only that one sound – those tiny stirrings and muffled pulses of an egg with an owl chick just beginning to grow.

The chick itself, a tiny speck, floated in the hugeness of the liquid sea contained within that egg, that Sacred Orb. Oh, she had planned it so carefully. The egg was to hatch on a night just as she'd hatched on: the night of a lunar eclipse. Nyra had been named for the Nyra of ancient legends, born when the moon dropped from the sky and rose in the face of a hatchling. It was said that when an owl was hatched on the night of an eclipse, an enchantment was cast upon that creature, a charm, and that this charm was either good and led to a greatness of spirit or was bad and led to great evil.

"Aaah," she sighed and cocked her head once more to be sure.

"They're coming!" Primrose gasped. The two owls peered in astonishment from the hole. There was no way that they could be seen, but it was as if the squadron headed by Nyra had pinpointed their exact location.

"We've got to get out of here," Eglantine said.

"Leave the egg!"

"No!" she shouted. "Never!"

The two young owls burst out of the hole.

"There they are!" shrieked Nyra.

"To the fire! To the fire! Eglantine, we must go back into the fire."

Eglantine knew Primrose was right. They didn't know how to fly in fire, not like the colliering chaw, but they were better at it than the Pure Ones and, more important, they could fight with fire – as expertly as the Pure Ones fought with battle claws.

The two young owls rose in the night and raced in flight towards the flame-scorched sky.

CHAPTER EIGHTEEN

"It Cannot fail!"

A gannet flying in the vicinity had pointed them in the direction that Gylfie and Digger were now flying. The gannet thought that he had seen something that might have been two owls flying low. So Gylfie and Digger were now skimming just above the ground. On occasion, Digger lighted down to walk, using his tracking skills to find any sign of the two missing owls. This was difficult work, for Digger was not simply looking for tracks of the two owls but 'tracks' of Soren's strange dream, as he had explained it to them. Ahead was a tree stump with a hole at its base. Could a hole be considered a clear space too? Digger knew that he might be prejudiced in this case. He was a Burrowing Owl after all, and Burrowing Owls lived in similar holes. Any ground cavity was always extremely attractive to an owl such as Digger. So he walked forwards a few paces. Suddenly he stopped in his tracks and blinked. Quivering on a low shrub next to the hole was a feather. Not just any feather. A Barn Owl's, and not just any Barn Owl's, but Eglantine's.

"What is it, Digger?" Gylfie asked, seeing that the Burrowing Owl had stopped.

"Eglantine has been here."

"No!" Gylfie said excitedly. "How can you be sure? I mean, how can you tell one Barn Owl feather from another?"

Digger gave the Elf Owl a withering gaze. "My friend, need I remind you that when Eglantine was first rescued all those months ago, I was the one who tracked her? I am more than familiar with Eglantine's plumage. And from the looks of it Primrose has been here too!" The Burrowing Owl plucked from another bush a short black feather, just like the ones that grew on the back of the head of a Pygmy Owl.

Gylfie lighted down beside him. "Bless my gizzard! That *is* a Barn Owl feather, judging by its neck band." Barn Owls were brown and white. Their faces and the front of their necks were all white.

"I'm going inside to explore," Digger announced. "You keep a lookout, all right?"

Seconds later, the Burrowing Owl called up from the hole. "They've been here for sure. Talon marks, pellets, a few more feathers." Digger paused. "And..."

"And what?" Gylfie was almost hopping with excitement.

"You're not going to believe this."

"What?"

"There is a mark here that could only have been made by one thing."

"What, for Glaux's sake?" By this point, Gylfie was almost jumping out of her feathers.

"An egg – a Barn Owl egg."

A stunned silence followed. Then Gylfie, recovering her senses, stuck her head into the hole and said out loud to no one in particular, "That can't be. Eglantine is too young."

"Who says it's Eglantine's?" Digger asked, crawling out of the hole. "There are other Barn Owls, as we know all too well."

Gylfie nodded and blinked. *All too well*, she thought.

"If you want to go in and see for yourself—" Digger offered.

Gylfie twisted her head no. Digger was one of the best in the tracking chaw, and this was exactly what the tracking chaw was trained to do: read the almost invisible signs left behind; the clues to where a lost owl might be; where a bobcat might have trodden; where crows might have mobbed and settled to peck away at their dying victim. But the mark of a single egg must indeed be one of the most subtle of all signs. What a cunning eye that Burrowing Owl had!

Gylfie looked overhead. She could spot Soren and the rest of the chaw. "We'd better go back and tell them." But she had hardly finished speaking when she saw a flame-coloured dart whistling down from the sky. It wasn't, however, a ball of fire. It was Ruby, the Short-eared Owl, who was a superb flier.

"Enemy spotted!" Ruby called out.

Digger and Gylfie spiralled up and followed Ruby to a cliff where the chaw had assembled.

"We found signs of a hole where Eglantine and Primrose have been," Digger said. But there was no time to report about the strange markings left by an egg.

"No idea where they were heading?" Ezylryb asked.

"We didn't have time to explore any further before Ruby came. But there was no blood. No signs of violence," Gylfie added and looked at Soren, who was shaking so hard she thought he might just tumble from his perch.

"Well, we've spotted a squadron of Pure Ones," Ezylryb said, "and they have not yet spotted us. So that gives us some advantage. I guess they are chasing Eglantine and Primrose. So if we can continue to follow them without being seen, so much the better."

Gylfie blinked. How could they follow them without being detected? Indeed, how could they follow them if two of the best scouts, Twilight and Ruby, were perched right here with the rest of them as was Sylvana, leader of the tracking chaw?

"Gannets," Ezylryb replied tersely, seeming to read Gylfie's mind.

Of course, thought Gylfie. *Gannets*. And who would know those seabirds better than Ezylryb?

Ezylryb knew all the ocean birds. The old Whiskered Screech, who came from the Northern Kingdoms and the land of the Great North Waters, was as close as an owl could get to being a seabird. Intimate of seagulls, gannets, shearwaters and cormorants, he knew their ways and they respected him and, more important, trusted him as they did no other land bird. So the gannets were scouting the Pure Ones for Ezylryb.

Suddenly the striking white wings tipped in black cut through the night.

"There he is!" said Soren. *Oh, maybe – just maybe – he's seen Eglantine. No blood, no signs of violence,* Soren kept repeating to himself what Gylfie had told him. He blinked and gripped with his talons the stone edge on which he was perched. Gannets were huge. This one's wingspan, Soren guessed, was more than a metre across. The bird glided on to the stone cliff with barely a wing flap.

Gannets are formal birds with many odd customs that involve the bowing and bobbing of their heads, the touching of their beaks in light clashes like swords crossing. With great deference this gannet stepped towards Ezylryb and extended his beak. Ezylryb did likewise, but because his beak was so much shorter, he had to take several steps forward. There was the click of the beaks clashing. This was the signal that conversation could begin.

"What have you to report, sir?" Ezylryb asked.

"Honourable Ezylryb of the Great North Waters and Stormfast Island. It is with great displeasure that I must bring you this news." The gannet's voice was a deep guttural croak.

"Go on," rasped Ezylryb.

"There is not one but two squadrons and an incoming platoon of Pure Ones."

"A platoon!" several of the owls said in stunned voices. A platoon was composed of at least four squadrons. They would be vastly outnumbered.

The gannet continued, "They are heading for the forest fire that still burns in the eastern regions of The Beaks."

"That seems odd. They aren't good in fire. Can't fight with fire. Why are they going there?"

"They are chasing two rather young owls – a Pygmy and a Barn Owl."

"Eglantine and Primrose!" Soren blurted out.

The gannet swung his head towards Soren and glared. "And," he continued, "the young owls were leading them there."

Now Barran spoke. "Tell me, sir. Do you think you were spotted?"

"Oh, most certainly. It is hard for white wings of my breadth to go unnoticed. As I am sure you must understand, being a Snowy yourself. But it is common for gannets to fly inland when there are forest fires near lakes. The flame glare on the lake makes fishing rather easy for us, and we do enjoy an occasional spot of lake fish. So I made sure to make a few feints at the lake to sustain the guise of casual fishing."

"Very smart." Ezylryb nodded and paused. Soren could tell that Ezylryb was thinking very hard because he had blinked his eyes shut and kept them that way for several seconds. Then he opened his eyes. The one held in the perpetual squint looked as it always did, completely unreadable and scary. The other eye had a gleam in it. "Thank you, sir, for your excellent reconnaissance." He paused again, and then added, almost as an afterthought, "And thank you for your use of the word 'feint'." Even the gannet looked puzzled by this.

Soren and Gylfie exchanged glances. Why in the world was Ezylryb thanking the gannet for a word?

"Always at your service, Honourable Ezylryb."

And then an equally elaborate sequence of bows and accompanying gestures commenced as the gannet took his leave. Soren watched him slide gracefully through the black night until the gleaming white wings were just slivers in the darkness.

"A squadron and a platoon," Barran said tensely. What was left unspoken was that they were up against an enemy that outnumbered them, and there was no Strix Struma to lead her Strikers into battle. Of course, they had originally thought that they were merely coming on a search-and-rescue mission, and since the fires had been spotted, the colliering chaw had decided to fly that night. In all, they had the search-and-rescue chaw, the tracking chaw, which always accompanied search-and-rescue, the colliering chaw, and then, of course, embedded within this assemblage of chaws was the Chaw of Chaws, composed of Soren, Gylfie, Twilight, Ruby, Martin, Digger and Otulissa. Each was a member of other chaws, but their uncanny ability to work together made them a fearsome fighting force.

"Yes indeed, a squadron and a platoon," Ezylryb said crisply. "We are outnumbered, but we are not outwitted." All the owls seemed to perch a little straighter; their feathers fluffed up a little more. What did the old ryb mean? "You might have wondered why I found that word 'feint' so... so... How should I put it... fetching?" He swivelled his head about and seemed to fix each owl in the yellow glare of his crinkled-up eye. "Because, that is precisely what we are going to do – create a feint. And not just a feint, but an immense illusion, the likes of which has never been seen. We number only a little more than twenty owls, but they will think we are hundreds."

"How is that, Ezylryb?" Barran asked, genuinely perplexed.

"All of those owls – the Pure Ones – are Barn Owls, are they not?"

Everyone nodded.

"And Barn Owls are known for what?" He looked directly at Soren. "Their hearing, of course. Their superb, unequalled ability to hear. We are going to get within range of the fire but still be undercover. We are going to divide up into three teams and peg-out as we used to say up in the Northern Kingdoms. I shall lead one peg, Barran shall lead one and, my dear, your estimable mate Boron" – he swung his head to the old Snowy monarch of the tree, who along with Barran led search-and-rescue – "will lead the third. The reason I have chosen the three of us is because we know the odd language of the Northern Kingdoms and the Great North Waters, for they were once home to all of us."

"I know a little bit too, Ezylryb," Otulissa piped up.

"Of course, wouldn't you know it?" Gylfie whispered to Soren. "The gift of the gab works in all languages."

"Yes, I do recall your study of the Northern Kingdoms for your mission into St Aggie's, my dear. That will be helpful." The previous winter, when the Chaw of Chaws had been sent on a special spy mission into St Aggie's, their cover story was that they had been blown off course up into the Northern

Kingdoms and then had fled. To be convincing, they had had to study a bit about this place that was so different from the Southern Kingdoms. Otulissa, of course, had overdone it. She had studied everything, including the language.

"It will not all be in Krakish, however. Some will be in Hoolian. We shall be giving information, or I should say misinformation, about troop positions, battle claws, and not just platoons – but divisions!"

Brilliant! Soren thought. Absolutely brilliant. And because they would sometimes be speaking in Krakish, the language of the Northern Kingdoms, the enemy would think that they had recruits from there. The owls of the Northern Kingdoms were thought to be the fiercest fighters on earth. It would scare the gizzards out of the Pure Ones. *Oh, I hope it works*, Soren fervently wished.

"It cannot fail!" thundered Ezylryb.

CHAPTER NINETEEN

The Peg-out

"Gishmahad frissah bralaag gyrrrmach tuoy oschuven..."

Nyra blinked in astonishment. It simply could not be! But it was. She was hearing it. The harsh sounds of ancient Krakish, a language now only spoken in the Northern Kingdoms, were crashing in her ear slits. Nyra herself had come from the Northern Kingdoms and still spoke and understood the language. A sublieutenant from her squadron had picked up on it and reported to her immediately. Smoke had grown thick once more, and they had lost the sky track of the Barn Owl and the Pygmy just before the sublieutenant, Uglamore, had appeared with the devastating news. She followed him to a safe tree upwind of the fire. Uglamore had reported that he had first picked up bits of Hoolian and then the language had become incomprehensible, but he had a feeling it might be Krakish.

"You did well in seeking me out," Nyra said. If there were Northern Kingdom owls in the vicinity and they were in league with the owls of the Great Ga'Hoole Tree, it could prove disastrous. For a few seconds she forgot about the Sacred Orb. She continued swivelling her head in small movements to scan by degrees the source of the conversation. As best as she could ascertain, there was a large group of owls somewhere to the northwest of the tree in which she was now perched. There were a number of safe trees in that direction that would offer refuge. Now she blinked again. Her head froze. "Division! They have a division!" she gasped. The owls surrounding her wilfed.

"Division Six requests sixty pairs of deep ice claws, forty-two standard battle claws."

"Sub-squadron Four requests additional colliers." Then from another tree there was a burst of Krakish.

Ezylryb suppressed his desire to laugh. It was a classic peg-out operation. Division Six and sub-squadron Four were entirely fictitious. They existed only in the ears and probably the gizzards of the enemy. To accomplish this, he had divided the Ga'Hoolian owls into three groups, stationing them in three different trees. The owls were then ordered to chatter about plans and weapons, troop positions and strategies. With this small yet elegant ruse, he might be able to deflect a significant number of the enemy from the trail of Primrose and Eglantine into the fire. Then the rest of the Pure Ones would have to fight in blazing forests, which was not the best terrain for them. Not all of the Ga'Hoolian owls were trained, as the colliering chaw was, to manoeuvre through towering flames, but they had all been required to do some work in fire conditions, and they were all proficient at fighting with burning branches.

The flame squadron, which was sometimes called the Bonk Brigade, was there. The Chaw of Chaws had been recruited for the flame squadron in the last battle with the Pure Ones. They were all here and a messenger had been sent back to the great tree to bring in every other fighting unit. Whether they would arrive in time was uncertain. *Who would ever have imagined when we set out to rescue two young owls that it would turn into this*, Ezylryb thought.

What if they found out we are a mere twenty-four owls without even one single battle claw between us!

Just then, Soren cocked his head and raised one toe of his left talon. This was the sign that Ezylryb had been waiting for. It meant that an enemy squadron was being split. Soren continued to listen. A second later, he raised two toes. This was what they had been waiting for. A platoon was being directed away from the fire! Only one and a half enemy squadrons were left. *Now that's a fair match,* Ezylryb thought. It was time for the action code to be given.

"The sea is dry. The puffins are perfect." Nyra blinked. Obviously it was a code she was hearing. She had ordered complete silence. She had now realised – but too late – that the owls of Ga'Hoole could hear her if they had a Barn Owl among them. Although so far she had heard only non-Barn Owl voices, and there had been a reference to Soren being back at the Island of Hoole. Now what could this code mean? There was no way she could possibly break it in the short time required. She felt it was best to stick to her plan of splitting the squadron; one half to go to the northwest front, which was some distance from the fire, and she would lead the remaining squadron into the fire. She had to get that egg back! If only

Kludd were here. But he had taken the best of their elite units south to St Aggie's.

With her lifted talon, she gave the signal to proceed with the plan of splitting the squadron and diverting the platoon to the northwest. Uglamore lifted off from the limb and soon Nyra did too, heading for the fire with her squadron and a half.

Meanwhile, high on a branch of a very tall larch tree, Primrose and Eglantine perched. Eglantine had propped herself in a V-shaped wedge where a branch joined the main trunk of the tree. She could therefore still hang on to the egg with her talons. Although the tree had thus far been untouched by the fire, she could feel the branches tremble from the onslaught of the hot gusts and intense thermal drafts that the forest fire created. Soren had said forest fires had their own private weather system and one had to learn how to ride the hot updrafts and cruise around something they called the heat band. All owls, when they reached a certain age, were supposed to do some training in each of the chaws even if it was not necessarily the one they had been assigned to. But neither Eglantine nor Primrose had reached that age yet. However, they had some training in flying with burning branches for torch fighting, which had been used to great effect against the Pure Ones.

Primrose crept out to the end of the branch.

"Any sign?" Eglantine asked by beaking the words silently. If Nyra was around, she didn't want her to hear anything that would give away their location. Primrose shook her head to indicate no. But it was not more than three seconds later that Eglantine heard her gasp and saw Primrose twist her head around and flip it back. Eglantine did the same. Overhead in combat formation were the Nyra Annihilators!

CHAPTER TWENTY

A Crown of Fire

"But look!" Eglantine shouted and then clamped her beak shut. She had been so excited at the sight of Soren flying out of a smoke bank and leading the Chaw of Chaws, with Bubo and the colliering chaw following, that she had forgotten and spoken aloud. In that instant, Nyra suddenly went into a steep, banking turn and headed directly towards the tree where Eglantine and Primrose were perched.

"To the fire! Leave the egg, Eglantine," Primrose screeched.

"No! Never!"

Egg! What egg? Then Soren remembered that Digger had found the imprint of an egg. Soren's mind was racing. His gizzard was aquiver with gladness and terror. Gladness that his sister was alive and terror as he saw Nyra head directly towards the sound of Eglantine's voice. Then he saw his sister and Primrose blast out of the branches of the larch tree and head directly towards the fire. *Genius! Little genius! She's leading them into the flame field, which she knows they cannot contend with as skilfully as we can. But can Eglantine and Primrose do it? They're so inexperienced.* The thought had barely passed through his mind when another slammed into it. It all made sense now. That egg. He saw Eglantine clutching it. It must be Nyra's egg!

"Very high stakes your sister plays with." Twilight slid in next to Soren.

"Where's Ezylryb?" Soren asked.

"Back with the Frost Beaks," Twilight replied. Soren had asked the question in all seriousness and had forgotten that Nyra and the other enemy Barn Owls could pick up on everything. How quick of Twilight to carry on the fiction of the Northern Kingdoms with a reference to the legendary 24th Frost Beaks Division, which Ezylryb himself had commanded.

Eglantine and Primrose had just sliced through the clear space between two blazing trees.

"Torch," Soren said. Otulissa and Ruby approached with burning branches in their beaks.

"Snap set one." At that, Bubo flew up and, having the strongest beak of all the owls, bit the two burning branches in half.

"Ignite," Soren ordered.

Martin, as the smallest of the colliering owls, flew in with a small, glowing, kindling twig and set fire to the ends of the newly broken branches. Now instead of two burning branches there were four.

"Snap set two." This time Poot, the first lieutenant in colliering, and Elvan, a Great Grey who was the colliering ryb, flew in with two more branches. Bubo repeated the action. Now there were eight. The burning branches multiplied exponentially.

Soon they were all armed and flying. So far, the colliering chaw and the Chaw of Chaws had performed flawlessly, meshing their particular skills, their actions, and their manoeuvres in perfect harmony.

Soren gave the next order. "Round out." With those words, the Chaw of Chaw split and flew into formation for a bilateral attack on Nyra's squadron.

Nyra saw them coming in. She felt the terror in her squadrons' gizzards. "The Sacred Orb!" she screamed. "Cowards will have their eyes pecked out!" At that moment, Ruby struck. Nyra did not turn her head, but she heard a rearguard owl plummet from the formation towards the ground. Then she felt a stillness in the air beside her as Uglamore went yeep. She dove after him and gave him a sharp jab with her beak. "Mooncalf!" Nyra shreed in the high-pitched wail of a Barn Owl. To be called a mooncalf, which meant both idiot and coward, was the worst insult a commander could throw at a soldier. But the jab and the insult did the trick. At twenty feet, Uglamore recovered before hitting the ground, and now they all pressed on with new vigour in their chase after Eglantine and Primrose.

"We're leading them on a merry," Eglantine whispered. It was what Soren and Martin had done in the last battle of the siege when they had lured Nyra into a tight space. But this space was not just tight, it was hot and they were getting bounced around fiercely by the tumultuous drafts of the burning forest. Behind a curtain of flames, they had both spotted a safe tree. If only they could get there and lose Nyra and her squadron! *Look for a hole in the flame curtain. Soren told me there were holes. If not a hole a tear, a nick. Anything will do*, Eglantine thought.

There it was! There it was! "Charge!" Eglantine yelled, and they both zipped through the opening, which closed behind them almost immediately and singed some of Primrose's tail feathers. But they were on the other side. And there was a tree. Not as safe as their last tree, for it was smouldering at its base, but it would do for now.

They had barely lighted down on a top branch with Eglantine propped as before, guarding the egg, when Nyra and her squadron burst through. But coming around from the other end with burning branches was the Chaw of Chaws.

Eglantine's eyes were fastened on Twilight who, in a flame-clear space, was advancing on Nyra.

Backing him up was Soren with not one but two burning branches – one held in his beak and the other in his talons.

Martin was looping in and out of the Ga'Hoole owls and igniting their branches with a small twig. Ruby was flying at high speed directly through the enemy squadron and making them scatter. But above the crackling and hissing of the fire, Twilight's voice could be heard. He had begun one of his battle chants.

You smokin' now,
You moonfaced owl.
These flames gonna make you howl.

You gonna skitter
Back to where you from.
And now you think you ain't so dumb?
Well, just let me tell you this –
You dumb as a fish,
Dumb as a snail,
Dumb as a rock,
And I shall prevail!

Nyra seemed confused and stunned. She had never before encountered Twilight, whose battle chants were in their own way as sharp and deadly as any battle claw. She had heard about this chant-talking owl and never understood how it could so disarm other owls. *But I am not other owls. I want my chick, my baby, my Sacred Orb.* And above her Nyra heard the heartbeats of two owls high in a tree.

Then everything happened so quickly that Eglantine and Primrose could not see what was coming or understand the words being yelled. Nyra had somehow avoided Twilight's swipe with the burning branch and had flown up as if she were flying directly towards Eglantine and Primrose. Primrose screamed something, but now the Pygmy Owl was no longer there. Had Nyra killed her? Why was she, Eglantine, standing on this branch all by herself still clutching the egg?

And now their voices from the flames were coming to her.

It was Soren's voice. "Drop the egg! Drop the egg."

"I can't! I can't! It gives us power, Soren. Power!"

Then she heard a sterner voice. *Great Glaux. It's Boron.*

"Drop the egg. That is a command!"

But their voices were now very dim in Eglantine's head. Her gizzard stilled, her eyes fixed on the most beautiful sight she had ever seen. Flames leaping joyfully, freely, they wound like the most gorgeous banners into the blackness of the night. For the conflagration that raged around her was pulling the deadliest trick of all. Eglantine was flame dazed and halfway to being completely fire blinked. She saw only beauty. She felt no heat. The fire was leaping from treetop to treetop. Eglantine's treetop was next.

"It's crowning," Soren yelled in a hoarse voice. "It's crowning, Eglantine. You'll be burned alive!"

CHAPTER TWENTY-ONE

The Gollymopes

Nyra looked at the shattered fragments of eggshell at her feet. She nudged them gently with her talon.

"Your Pureness, we must move on. There is a rolling bed of embers moving towards us. And the tree" – Uglamore looked up at the tree from which the egg had dropped – "It's about to fall. There will be more eggs in the future, Your Pureness, rest assured."

"I am assured but I shall not rest. And I vow to kill Eglantine if it is the last thing I ever do." Her once-white face was almost black now with soot. She flapped her wings once, twice, and rose in the air. "Kill! Kill! Kill Eglantine, the betrayer, murderer of the Sacred Orb!"

When she had composed herself, Nyra turned to Uglamore. "Where have they all gone? There was an entire division. How can they just vanish?" They were flying west towards the distant lands known as Beyond the Beyond where the Pure Ones had secured a stronghold.

"Uh..." Uglamore hesitated. He had known this moment would come and he had a response prepared. But he was nervous. "Well, Your Pureness, they know how to fly in fires, these owls of Ga'Hoole. There is nothing like them. They can hide behind flame curtains and find passageways through them that we cannot."

"Hmmm," Nyra replied.

He cast a nervous glance at her. Maybe she believed him. It sounded reasonable. There was no way that he would ever tell her the truth: that it had all been a ruse, that they had been tricked, that seventy-five owls had been outwitted and outmanoeuvred by a mere twenty-four owls – and none with battle claws! It gave Uglamore pause. Was it possible, he thought, that the Great Ga'Hoole Tree could produce a better soldier than the Pure Ones?

Kludd and Nyra and Stryker, the second in overall command, had trained them to fight magnificently. They were better armed than any other group of owls.

Their discipline was the best. They were the best! Already they had conquered more territory than any other owl army, save perhaps those of the Northern Kingdoms. There was no discipline in the Great Ga'Hoole Tree. Every owl knew that. Those owls were free to do anything – anything at all! Then it suddenly struck Uglamore – a free society of owls might, in fact, produce a very fine soldier despite the lack of discipline. Discipline counted, but it had not won this battle. Wits had. *When was the last time I used my wits? When was the last time anyone ever listened to me? When was the last time I really had any kind of an idea about anything?*

Nyra banked across the headwind that was making a direct course to Beyond the Beyond hard to hold. Uglamore followed, as did the rest of the platoon.

"So Octavia," Ezylryb settled on to his favourite parlour perch in his hollow and plucked a dried caterpillar from a small dish, his favourite snack food. "Our young Guardians, the Chaw of Chaws, have become quite proficient in torch fighting. Simply amazing what they can do with a blazing branch. I mean, we have always had a flame squadron. But it was a rather minor unit and they only used burning branches defensively, never offensively as these young owls did. They have essentially invented a new weapon."

"Yes sir, that they did," said the plump, elderly nest-maid snake, as she dusted off the piles of books. "Very inventive those young owls."

"Yes, I suppose they are the fruits of an open free-thinking society."

"Nothing wrong with that, sir," Octavia replied.

"No, nothing at all."

Octavia, however, could tell that something was wrong by the tone in Ezylryb's voice.

"But don't you think it's rather ironic that years ago I hung up my battle claws, hid them away in that back chamber of the hollow? And now something even more destructive, more deadly than battle claws has been invented, not to mention the flecks. Glaux, those flecks are dangerous."

"Yes sir, that they are." Octavia knew that Ezylryb was, as he was sometimes inclined to do, approaching by a very circuitous route the heart of what was troubling him. And after all these years of serving her master, she knew what part she had to play. "Tell me, sir, did you pick up a fire branch in this most recent skirmish?"

The old Whiskered Screech fixed her in his squinted gaze. Octavia could feel the penetrating stare. I swear he sees more with that old squinty eye than any owl with two good ones.

"Now, what do you think, Octavia?"

Octavia laughed. "I know you, sir. I don't think you touched one burning branch. You were telling them how to peg-out, jabbering away in Krakish, and so on."

"And so on," Ezylryb churred good-naturedly. "But it gives one pause," he continued.

"Pause about what, sir?" Octavia was now straightening out the papers on his desk.

"Does it not strike you as odd that fire was always used for constructive things – cooking, making light for candles to read by, and not as offensive weapons?"

"Battle claws!" Octavia interrupted. "What about them? You don't cook with battle claws, sir. And to make them you need fire."

"Just so, my dear. You've got me there. But the owls' excitement about fighting with torches unnerves me somewhat. Boron and Barran are now instituting new training classes for the flame squadron." Ezylryb did not sound particularly happy about this.

"Well, we have to get with the times, don't we, sir?"

"What if we don't like the times?" he said petulantly.

Octavia stopped dusting, coiled up, swung her head towards him and fixed him with her sightless eyes.

How does she do it? Ezylryb thought. *She sees straight through me with no eyes at all!*

"Sir, don't go into a gollymope on me, getting the dismals and all that nonsense," Octavia spoke brusquely to her master.

"Yes, yes, of course not. I must get to the parliament chamber. We are convening tonight."

"Tonight? It's a celebration, sir."

"For some." He paused. "Not for Dewlap."

"Oh dear. Still out of sorts, is she?"

"Out of sorts is putting it nicely. She's a Glaux-forsaken mess!"

Meanwhile, in another part of the Great Ga'Hoole Tree, there was an owl on the brink of a major gollymope. Otulissa bent over a plan she had made, a landing diagram for an attack on the Pure Ones. *And now the divisions actually exist. And there really will be a platoon of Frost Beaks from the Northern Kingdoms!* She sighed. It was hopeless. If only someone would listen to her – Ezylryb, Boron, Barran – even Bubo. The sounds of the celebration welcoming back Eglantine and Primrose drifted into her hollow.

Madame Plonk flew by on an unsteady course. She had obviously had too much of the milkberry brew that the adults often drank at celebrations.

"Am I the only one with an ounce of sense around here?" Otulissa said out loud to no one in particular.

"Hardly!"

Otulissa's head spun around. She gasped as she saw Ezylryb poking his beak into her hollow. "I want you, Eglantine, and the band – no one else – down in the parliament chamber in a quarter of an hour."

Otulissa blinked in utter bewilderment. *What in the world?*

"And Otulissa, try to be discreet when you fetch them. Don't go beaking off in your usual voluble style!"

"Well… well… no, of course not, sir." But she could have sworn she saw his squinted eye wink.

CHAPTER TWENTY-TWO

The Living Dead

The Boreal Owl who stood guard at the entrance to the parliamentary chambers nodded for them to go in. The young owls had been here only twice before, and each and every one of them now felt a tad shameful about all the times they had eavesdropped on the parliament. The members of parliament were arranged in their usual positions on a slender white birch-tree branch that had been bent into a semicircle. There was, of course, one vacant spot on this perch: the space that Dewlap had once occupied. But then all the young owls gasped as they simultaneously realised that the pile of dirty grey feathers in the corner of the chamber was attached to a bird, and that bird was the owl Dewlap. What in Glaux's name had happened to her? She had once been a rich, lustrous brown colour, shot through with steaks of white. But all of her brown feathers had turned grey and her amber eyes had turned the colour of mud. Her head jerked in palsied movements and she seemed to be muttering something unintelligible.

Boron spoke first. His voice was gentle. He realised what a shock this was for the young owls and he fervently hoped that this notion of the old Whiskered Screech's was right. The band and Otulissa and Eglantine were bold. There was no doubt about that. But were they really mature enough for this? "Young'uns, she is not shattered. This has nothing to do with flecks," the Snowy monarch said softly.

"What then?" Twilight asked in a barely audible voice.

"Her gizzard has grown still," Boron continued. "And her heart is broken."

"Broken?" asked Gylfie. The young owls had never heard of such a thing as a broken heart.

"This is difficult to explain," Boron said, looking at each of them and at the same time wondering how he would do it. "We owls experience most of our strongest emotions, as you all know, in our gizzards, but there are a few reserved for the heart. When an owl has been unfaithful, has betrayed a cause or a friend or, like Dewlap, the entire tree as she did by leaking information to the enemy during the siege, it has also betrayed its own heart. When such an owl realises what it has done, its gizzard often becomes still and its heart tries to work harder to make up for the difference. But an owl's heart cannot do what an owl's gizzard is supposed to do, and it breaks. Not literally, but it breaks in a way that even though it still pumps blood, its spirit is broken."

"What happens to such an owl?" Soren asked in a scared voice.

"Well, it becomes rather like its heart and gizzard. It grows still. It continues to eat and breathe, but it is helpless. It is as if the owl's soul, its scroomsaw, has left its body, yet it is not dead. The owl is not a scroom. It is what we call the living dead." The young owls were very quiet. They could not even imagine such a thing, but when they looked at Dewlap, they could believe it.

"So what do you do?" Otulissa asked in a quiet voice.

"Well, my dear, that is where you come in." And the way Boron said 'you', it seemed that he meant Otulissa in particular. "We have a mission for you."

"Me?" Otulissa asked.

"You, Otulissa, with the help of your friends here."

"What is it?" she asked. Soren could see that Otulissa was trembling.

"Be gentle," Boron replied. Now all of the young owls blinked in confusion. Perhaps the most confused was Twilight. *Be gentle? That's a mission? You gotta be kidding!*

"We, the parliament of the Great Ga'Hoole Tree, are charging you six owls" – and this time Boron was sure to also look at Eglantine – "with the mission of delivering Dewlap to the Retreat of the Glauxian Sisters, in the Northern Kingdoms, on the Island of Elsemere, in the Everwinter Sea."

Otulissa was stunned beyond belief. How could this be? She had dreamed forever of going to the Northern Kingdoms to find fighting owls, to see the magnificent snowy landscapes and cliffs of ice. But to be sent there as an attendant to a feeble old owl, whom she hated and blamed for the death of her beloved Strix Struma – it was too much! Simply too much. She staggered slightly on the perch, but Twilight extended a steadying wing. For the first time in her life, Otulissa was speechless. Indeed, this was a situation beyond words.

Just then, there was a rap on the parliament door. The Boreal Owl stuck his head in.

"Permission to enter, your honours? The new slipgizzle from the eastern Barrens has arrived with an urgent message."

"Permission granted."

A rather disreputable-looking Great Horned, missing one ear tuft, flew into the chamber.

"Your honours, I bring you ill tidings."

"Go on." Boron nodded.

"The Pure Ones took the canyons last eve. St Aggie's has fallen."

It was as if all the air had been sucked out of the chamber. The words blurred in Soren's ears. There was something said about Kludd and the 32nd regiment. Skench was wounded or killed? It was a hodgepodge of disjointed noises.

The young owls had been quickly dismissed. They thought they had been dismissed for good in view of the crisis, but just as they were filing out of the chamber, Ezylryb had called out to the Boreal Owl to have the young ones wait in the antechamber.

So they waited, but few words were exchanged for the first several minutes.

"St Aggie's fallen? What does it mean?" Soren spoke almost in a daze. In fact, they all seemed dazed, except for Digger.

"It means," the Burrowing Owl said in a hushed voice tight with fear, "the Pure Ones have control of the largest supply of flecks on earth."

"I still don't understand why I have to fly escort to that pathetic old owl," Otulissa whimpered.

Digger whirled round. "Get a grip Otulissa! You're worrying about flying Dewlap to the Northern Kingdoms. Meanwhile, the Pure Ones have control of all the flecks, and we now know what flecks can do! What does it mean, Soren asked. I'll tell you what it means. It means more shatterings. It means that the Pure Ones can gain control of our brains, our minds. It means we might never be able to think again. It means it would be better to die than become a mindless tool for the most destructive owls on earth. That's what it means, Otulissa."

The other four owls were astounded. Digger, usually subdued, philosophical and armed with endless patience, had suddenly become enraged. While the other owls had wilfed at the news that the Pure Ones had triumphed over St Aggie's, and appeared exceedingly slender with their feathers lying close to their bodies, Digger had puffed up and seemed almost twice his normal size as he spat out his rage at Otulissa.

The Boreal Owl now came into the antechamber. "Young'uns, the parliament would like to see you again. Follow me, please."

Once more, the six owls filed into the parliament chamber and took their places facing the curved birch branch where the members perched. They all noticed that Dewlap had been removed from the chamber. This time Barran began to speak.

"As you know young'uns, our situation is grave. We have won two battles, one last winter during the siege and now in the rescue of Eglantine and Primrose. But we have not won the war, which has turned more deadly than ever. We do not know how many of the St Aggie's troops have been conscripted into Kludd's army of the Pure Ones. But we must assume the worst; that the Pure Ones' ranks have grown. Therefore, Ezylryb would now like to talk to you about a second mission."

Ezylryb flew to the centre of the birch branch. "You are young, bold owls. You shall be journeying to the land of my hatching in the Northern Kingdoms. The land of the Great North Waters. Your journey was only to be one of mercy, of caring, as you gently escorted this sick and broken Burrowing Owl to the Glauxian Sisters on the Isle of Elsemere."

Soren felt Otulissa stir beside him. *She's hoping to get out of this, but it's not going to happen.* Soren could tell something else was coming.

"That is still your mission," Ezylryb continued.

Soren stole a look at Otulissa. Her beak was set in a most unbecoming fashion. He wasn't sure if it was anger or disappointment.

"But after you have completed the safe delivery of Dewlap, there is more we would like you to do..."

CHAPTER TWENTY-THREE

The Passing of the Claws

There was more. A lot more! Soren remained awake long after the other members of the band fell asleep. His mind kept running over the tasks they had been given. The enormity of the undertaking was mind-boggling. Otulissa and Gylfie were to go to the Glauxian Brothers Retreat to find another copy of the fleckasia book in their library. Soren, Twilight and Digger were to proceed to the Firth of Fangs in the most northwestern region of the Everwinter Sea and seek out an old warrior named Moss and then continue on to Stormfast Island, in the Bay of Kiel, to talk to a relative of Octavia's, a Kielian snake called Hoke of Hock. And finally, they were to go to Dark Fowl Island, where the legendary blacksmith Orf crafted the finest battle claws ever known in the owl world.

It was the chance of a lifetime, a trip to the Northern Kingdoms to recruit owls and arms to battle the Pure Ones who now held St Aggie's. But then again how long might their lives last in this new and dangerous world? Otulissa, of course, was triumphant. Finally the elders had listened to her. This would be the first step in the invasion plan she had thought about for months, ever since the death of Strix Struma. Gylfie, although miffed at being sent to do research, was also excited. Eglantine was thrilled at being included at last. As Boron told her in a graceful and eloquent speech, she had more than proved herself. In an act of unsurpassable bravery she had collected and reassembled the fragments of her nearly shattered mind. Although she had failed to keep Nyra and Kludd's egg as hostage, her courage had never wavered. It was only at the last minute when the crown fire threatened to engulf her that she had let the egg fall and flown from the tree. When Soren thought of the look in Eglantine's eyes as Boron had described how courageous she'd been, well, he had never in his life been so proud.

But something is wrong with me, Soren thought. *Why am I not excited?* He looked over at Digger and Gylfie and Twilight sleeping, each with their own wonderful dreams of the great adventures ahead in the Northern Kingdoms. *And yet I am the one with starsight, the one who dreams about things that sometimes happen, but I cannot sleep and cannot dream.*

Finally Soren gave up trying to sleep. He lofted up to the edge of the sky port of the hollow and perched for a few minutes. The sun rode high in the sky on this late summer day. *Why not go to the library*, he thought. He spread his wings and lifted off towards the higher branches of the great tree to where the library hollow was. The world seemed too bright at this hour of the day, especially as he rose higher to where the branches of the great tree were sparser. The dimness of the library was welcoming, and the change from the brightness to the shadows made him blink as his eyes adjusted. So it was several seconds before he realised that within the shadows there was a denser darkness in the corner, at the desk reserved for Ezylryb. This was so unexpected that Soren blurted out, "What are you doing here?"

Ezylryb churred softly, "I might ask the same of you, young'un."

"I couldn't sleep."

"Come to my hollow Soren. I have something for you."

"Yes sir."

The two owls left the library and flew to a sky port on the northwest side of the tree. Octavia was draped over a nearby branch. She swung her head towards Ezylryb. "Be wanting your tea now, sir?"

"That would be lovely, Octavia. Yes thank you."

As they entered the hollow, Soren blinked again rapidly to adjust his vision. This time it was not a shadow within the dimness that caught his eye but something gleaming with a bright intensity. His gizzard gave a quiver of excitement. In the middle of Ezylryb's tea table were the battle claws made on Dark Fowl Island – the very same battle claws that Gylfie and Soren had first seen the previous autumn when Ezylryb had disappeared, and they had gone into his hollow to snoop for possible clues. Except at that time the claws had been rusty with age and were hung in a secret compartment of the hollow. Now they had been polished to a shimmering radiance. They absolutely glowed on the table. It was almost as if they were a living, breathing thing and not just finely tempered metal.

Soren was dumbfounded. He had thought no one was to know about these battle claws. He cautiously moved around the table, almost mesmerised by the gleaming claws. "What is this all about?"

"It is about you, lad."

"Me?" Now he was genuinely bewildered.

"They are for you, Soren. Call it, if you will, a passing of the claws."

"But why me, Ezylryb?"

"For many reasons really, but first and foremost, you are the leader of the band."

"But when we go to the Northern Kingdoms, it's really Otulissa's mission. She is the one who knows the most. She even speaks their language."

"There are many kinds of knowing, Soren. Otulissa has one kind and you have another. With these claws Moss, Hoke of Hock and the smith on Dark Fowl will all know that you are truly an emissary from Ezylryb, once known as Lyze of Kiel. They are your passport, your safe-conduct permit. The claws are, if you will, the keys to the Northern Kingdoms."

"The keys to the Northern Kingdoms," Soren spoke in a whispery voice.

"Every owl will know that you are my ward."

"Ward?" Soren tore his eyes from the radiance of the claws and looked up at Ezylryb. "Your ward?"

Soren wasn't even sure if he knew what the word meant.

"You are under my protection as a son would be."

"As your son?"

"It is not that complicated, Soren. You have no parents. I have no children. You are my ward now, but with that comes certain responsibilities, one of them being to represent not only me but also the other owls of the Great Ga'Hoole Tree."

"Ready for tea, sir? And I managed to snitch some milkberry buns from Cook." Octavia slithered into the hollow with the tea things on her back.

"Yes, do come in. I think our Soren here is a bit overcome."

"Oh my, my." Octavia flicked her tongue. "Oh dear lad, how hard I worked polishing those claws for you. They were a bit rusty, as you might recall." She slid her head sideways towards Soren, and Soren gasped. Had she told Ezylryb how he and Gylfie had snooped around last autumn? The old snake laughed, and Ezylryb joined her.

Soren blinked. *Well if she has, I guess no one thinks it's that awful.*

Soren ate his tart and sipped his tea in a bewildered state, unable to take his eyes off the battle claws. It suddenly occurred to him that he had no place to keep them.

"Sir, we don't leave until the eve after this one. Where shall I keep them?"

"I shall keep them for you until then. Don't worry."

But Soren was worried. How would he explain all this to the rest of the band, and Otulissa and Eglantine? Suddenly however, he was quite sleepy. Too sleepy to worry. He tried to stifle a yawn.

"Getting sleepy, dear?" Octavia said.

"Yes, a bit I guess."

"Well..." – Ezylryb peered out the sky port – "the sun is still pretty high. I would say that you have a good several hours until dusk and tween time. Why don't you fly along and get some rest?"

"Yes, I think I will, sir." Soren flapped up to the sky port and just before taking off, he turned and said, "Thank you, Octavia, for the tea and tart. And thank you, Ezylryb." He paused. "For everything."

Octavia had cleared up the tea things and slithered out of the hollow. She knew when her master wanted to be alone. It was not the gollymopes this time, however, at least not exactly. The old Whiskered Screech just needed to be alone. That was all.

The arthritis in his starboard wing was kicking up again. Always did this time of year. He'd pluck himself a quill from his port wing although the starboard one always offered the best. He winced as he pulled a new pinfeather. He sat down at his desk and took out a piece of his finest parchment, dipped the quill in an inkwell and began to write.

The time has come,
The claws are passed.
An old owl rests,
A die's been cast.
It is a war for heart, gizzard and mind.
The weapons they wield, more deadly than mine.
A blade draws blood,
A fire burns.
But with the flecks,
A mind unlearns,
A soul unhinges,
And then a gizzard quakes and cringes.
Senses dull,
Reason scatters.
The heart grows numb,
An owl shatters.
But these six owls are strong and bold,
And their story has not yet been told.

Ezylryb put down his quill. He turned his head. The red tinge of the setting sun cast an eerie light on the battle claws that now seemed to glow with the heat of a blacksmith's fire. He reached out with his mangled talon and touched the claws. It was almost as if he could still feel the scorching heat of the fire in which they had been wrought. *My Glaux,* he thought, *what am I sending these owls into? What hagsmire awaits them?*

What hagsmire awaits owlkind?

THE OWLS

and others from Guardians of Ga'Hoole

The Shattering

THE BAND

SOREN: Barn Owl, *Tyto alba,* from the Forest Kingdom of Tyto; escaped from St Aegolius Academy for Orphaned Owls; training to be a Guardian at the Great Ga'Hoole Tree

GYLFIE: Elf Owl, *Micranthene whitneyi,* from the Desert of Kuneer; escaped from St Aegolius Academy for Orphaned Owls; Soren's best friend; training to be a Guardian at the Great Ga'Hoole Tree

TWILIGHT: Great Grey Owl, *Strix nebulosa,* free flier, orphaned within hours of hatching; training to be a Guardian at the Great Ga'Hoole Tree

DIGGER: Burrowing Owl, *Speotyto cunicularius,* from the Desert of Kuneer; lost in the desert after attack in which his family was killed by owls from St Aegolius; training to be a Guardian at the Great Ga'Hoole Tree

THE LEADERS OF THE GREAT GA'HOOLE TREE

BORON:
Snowy Owl, *Nyctea scandiaca,* the King of Hoole

BARRAN:
Snowy Owl, *Nyctea scandiaca,* the Queen of Hoole

EZYLRYB:
Whiskered Screech Owl, *Otus trichopsis*, the wise weather-interpretation and colliering ryb (teacher) at the Great Ga'Hoole Tree; Soren's mentor (also known as Lyze of Kiel)

STRIX STRUMA:
Spotted Owl, *Strix occidentalis*, the dignified navigation ryb at the Great Ga'Hoole Tree; killed during siege of the great tree

DEWLAP:
Burrowing Owl, *Speotyto cunicularius*, the Ga'Hoolology ryb at the Great Ga'Hoole Tree; betrayed the great tree during the siege by the Pure Ones

SYLVANA: Burrowing Owl, *Speotyto cunicularius*, a young ryb at the Great Ga'Hoole Tree; head of the tracking chaw

OTHERS AT THE GREAT GA'HOOLE TREE

OTULISSA: Spotted Owl, *Strix occidentalis*, a student of prestigious lineage at the Great Ga'Hoole Tree

MARTIN: Northern Saw-whet Owl, *Aegolius acadicus*, in Ezylryb's chaw with Soren

RUBY: Short-eared Owl, *Asio flammeus*, in Ezylryb's chaw with Soren

EGLANTINE: Barn Owl, *Tyto alba,* Soren's younger sister

PRIMROSE: Pygmy Owl, *Glaucidium californicum*, Eglantine's best friend

MADAME PLONK: Snowy Owl, *Nyctea scandiaca,* the elegant singer of the Great Ga'Hoole Tree

BUBO: Great Horned Owl, *Bubo virginianus*, the blacksmith of the Great Ga'Hoole Tree

MRS PLITHIVER: Blind snake, formerly the nest-maid for Soren's family; now a member of the harp guild at the Great Ga'Hoole Tree

OCTAVIA: Kielian snake, nest-maid for Madame Plonk and Ezylryb

GINGER: Barn Owl, *Tyto alba*, formerly of the Pure Ones; now reformed and sharing Eglantine's sleeping hollow at the Great Ga'Hoole Tree

THE PURE ONES

KLUDD: Barn Owl, *Tyto alba,* Soren and Eglantine's older brother; leader of the Pure Ones (also known as Metal Beak and High Tyto)

NYRA: Barn Owl, *Tyto alba,* Kludd's mate

STRYKER: Barn Owl, *Tyto alba,* a Pure Guard lieutenant

UGLAMORE: Barn Owl, *Tyto alba*, a Pure Guard sublieutenant under Nyra

LEADERS OF ST AEGOLIUS ACADEMY FOR ORPHANED OWLS

SKENCH: Great Horned Owl, *Bubo virginianus*, the Ablah General of St Aegolius Academy for Orphaned Owls

SPOORN: Western Screech Owl, *Otus kennicottii,* first lieutenant to Skench

OTHER CHARACTERS

SIMON: Brown Fish Owl, *Ketupa (Bubo) zeylonensis,* a pilgrim owl of the Glauxian Brothers of the Northern Kingdoms

THE ROGUE SMITH OF SILVERVEIL: Snowy Owl, *Nyctea scandiaca,* a blacksmith not attached to any kingdom in the owl world, and sister of Madame Plonk

Read a sneak preview of the next book
in the Guardians of Ga'Hoole series,

The Burning

The pure ones have taken St Aggies, and if they
are not stopped soon they will launch another,
more deadly attack on the great tree. Can
Soren and the band recruit more allies in time?

"The name disturbs me," Digger said, looking down at the narrow finger of water they were following.

"What name?" Soren asked.

"This place where we are – the Firth of Fangs. Fangs… well, you know – none of us has the fondest memories of them."

"Oh, that bobcat," Twilight replied dismissively. When the band of four had been on their long journey to the Great Ga'Hoole Tree, they had a most unfortunate encounter with a fiendishly ravenous bobcat. Digger, Soren and Gylfie had never seen such long and horrible fangs. Twilight, however, claimed to have seen many in his day. Having been orphaned almost immediately after hatching, Twilight had brought himself up, taught himself how to fly, and lived a lifetime full of awesome danger and adventure almost before he had even moulted his first set of feathers.

"That bobcat, you say? I seem to remember, Twilight, that you didn't exactly find it a soothing experience," Soren spoke up now. Sometimes Soren found Twilight's complete denial of fear more irritating than his boasting.

"Not soothing, exactly," Twilight replied, "but I can't think of the word right now."

"Bracing, perhaps? Stimulating?" Digger said. "As in 'gets your blood going, sends a refreshing quiver through the old gizzard'?"

"Exactly. That's it!" Twilight replied, and Soren thought that Digger was sometimes just too nice.

"Well, let me tell you," Digger continued. "There is scant difference between a bracing feeling and a terrifying one. Fangs more than six inches long scare the be-Glaux out of me. And I cannot help but think that this Firth of Fangs place must have been named that for a reason. I only hope that the trip to seek out Moss, this old warrior friend of Ezylryb's, will be worth it."

"Well Digger," Eglantine, who had been flying in between Twilight and the Burrowing Owl, began to speak quietly, "technically a firth is a long narrow body of water, an indentation in the seacoast."

"Good grief! If I didn't know better I would have thought it was Otulissa speaking. No Eglantine, it's not the 'firth' part that bothers me. It's definitely the 'fang' part."

"But have you ever considered, Digger, that the firth might be called a fang because it is long and curved like a fang?" Eglantine flew closer to him as she posed the question.

"Oh, that's a thought. Its shape..."

But before the Burrowing Owl could look to confirm this, Soren let loose with a gizzard-piercing shriek as only a Barn Owl can.

"What is it?" Digger said. But then they all saw where Soren was looking – straight down. Several late-summer ice floes that had broken off the winter pack ice bobbed peacefully in the waters of the firth. But from one ice floe, clearly visible in the moonlight, gushed a stream of blood. An immense white beast like none they had ever seen was tearing something apart. It tipped its head back. Its immense fangs were bright with blood, and in its claws it held the squirming body of a seal.

"Want to say hello to those fangs Twilight?" Digger asked. "And with those claws it might provide a truly bracing experience!" The fangs were clearly longer than six inches.

Eglantine cried. "Look, I think that seal's baby is crying on the next floe! We've got to help that poor thing!"

"Mammish! Mammish!" wailed the small grey seal.

"We've gotta help!" Eglantine cried again. Soren's sister, Eglantine, the youngest and least experienced of all the owls, began a spiralling descent towards the floe where the baby seal wailed. The others followed.

But by the time they arrived, she was already standing on the floe trying to calm the baby.

"It doesn't speak Hoolian, and I can't remember any Krakish," Eglantine said rather desperately.

"Umm, umm..." Soren was grasping for the proper Krakish words. How he wished Otulissa were here. She was the only one who was fluent. The rest of them could manage only a few choppy phrases and random words. But Soren began. "Baby be all right! Baby be all right!" He looked around anxiously. The flow of blood from the seal's mother had dyed the water around them red. Twilight was transfixed. "I think it's a bear – a white bear."

"A polar bear?" Digger asked.

"Yes, that's it, I think," Twilight said.

"Oh Great Glaux," Digger sighed. "Now we know why this place is called the Firth of Fangs. I've read that polar bears are the biggest carnivores on Earth."

"And we are a floating meat market here," Soren said tensely as the floe with the bear drifted closer and closer.

"They are swimmers too – powerful swimmers," Digger said with a tremor in his voice.

"But can they fly?" Twilight said. "I suggest we get out of here quickly."

"But what about the baby?" Eglantine said in a pleading voice. The baby was now making quite a racket. "We can't leave the baby." Eglantine was crying almost as hard as the baby seal.

Suddenly there was a tremendous bump and the owls and the seal skidded to the other edge of the ice floe. The polar bear's floe had crashed into them. The bear stopped gorging for the moment and lifted its face. In the moonlight it was an awesome sight. Its pure white muzzle was now stained with blood. It tipped its head back. "Arrrrraggggh!" It was a roar that shook the ice, the sea, not to mention the owls' gizzards.

Printed by RR Donnelley at Glasgow, UK